DUEL

DUEL

by Borys Antonenko-Davydovych

Translated by Yuri Tkacz

Originally published in Ukrainian as "Smert" in 1928.

Edited by Oleh S. Ilnytzkyj

Introduction © 1986, heirs of Dmytro Chub

© 2022, Cover image by Max Mendor

English translation © 2022, Yuri Tkacz

© 2022, Glagoslav Publications

www.glagoslav.com

ISBN: 978-1-911414-84-1

A catalogue record for this book is available from the British Library.

Published in English by Glagoslav Publications in August 2022.

BORYS ANTONENKO-DAVYDOVYCH

DUEL

TRANSLATED BY YURI TKACZ

GLAGOSLAV PUBLICATIONS

CONTENTS

BORYS ANTONENKO-DAVYDOVYCH

(1899-1984)

For life one pays only with blood,
Death can only be overcome with death.
                                        Vasyl Ellan

INTRODUCTION

Borys Antonenko-Davydovych (1899-1984) belongs to that colourful group of post-revolutionary writers who resurrected Ukrainian literature. He was born in 1899 in Romny, Poltava Province, into the family of an engine-driver. Before the 1917 revolution he had already finished his secondary education, and later studied at Kyiv University and the people's Institute of Education. In 1920, during the times of militant Communism, he took part in the battles against the anarchist Makhno. Shortly thereafter he headed the Education Department in Okhtyrka, later working in publishing houses and at the Kyiv Cinema Plant.

Antonenko-Davydovych was not only a writer, but also a thorough expert of the Ukrainian language and a translator of books from Russian. Altogether he wrote 24 books. His better works have been reprinted in England, the USA and Australia, as well as being translated into English, Polish, Bulgarian and Russian. The author's early works included *Knights of the Absurd* (1924), *Dusty Silhouettes* (1925), *Took-Took* (1926), *Blue Strawflower* (1927), *Duel* (1928), *Throughout Ukraine* (1930), *The Wings of Flying Artem* (1933).

In 1934-37, during Russia's rout of Ukrainian culture, when 240 Ukrainian writers perished, Antonenko-Davydovych was sentenced to ten years hard labour in Krasnoyarsk, Siberia. He remained in exile for 21 years, and only returned to Kyiv in 1956, after his rehabilitation.

He resumed writing once more: *Behind the Curtain* (1961), *Mother's Word* (1964), *Selected Works* (1967), *From Near and Far* (1969), *How We Speak* (1970).

However the early 1970s again saw the resumption of arrests, trials and the persecution of Ukrainian patriotism. One hundred and thirty-two writers, artists and scholars signed a protest letter to the regime against the renewed destruction of Ukrainian culture. Antonenko-Davydovych was one of the signatories. From then on his works stopped being published. The KGB began to make frequent searches of his home, confiscating letters, books and manuscripts, and a campaign of attacks was launched in the press.

In the last years of his life he was a sick, hounded man, blind in one eye. His wife, whom he had married in exile, spent periods in psychiatric hospitals until her death in 1982. And two years later, in May 1984, Borys Antonenko-Davydovych himself passed away, his memoirs having been earlier confiscated by the KGB.

Duel (titled *Smert'* in the Ukrainian original) brought the author fame and recognition for his courageous and talented work, but at the same time it brought even greater misery, persecution, and finally – exile. The novel was first published in 1927 in the Kyiv magazine *Life and Revolution*. *Duel* looks at the life and activities of a Party organization during the period of militant Communism. The action takes place in a small provincial town, reminiscent of Okhtyrka, where the author worked in 1920-21. At the time young Borys was a member of the Ukrainian Communist Party, later liquidated in 1924 on orders from the Comintern. Thus the author was well acquainted with Party politics, the circumstances prevailing in the city and the countryside. *Duel* is interesting in that it has no fictional characters, some even retain their real names.

In those days the Party organization assumed control of all aspects of everyday life. The situation was quite tense – the city was surrounded by the hostile countryside, which had no desire to pay levies to the occupying Russian regime. Besides, insurgent bands were organized in the villages to fight the Soviet government.

The novel's central hero is Kost Horobenko, a former Ukrainian nationalist, who now plays an active role in Party life. He has crossed over to the Soviet side, accepted their platform, but his actions, his judgements of people and his thoughts reflect a sustained inconsistency, a constant struggle with his own conscience. He is forever tormented by doubts. The villages had been the base of Ukrainianism, but now he has to venture there with others to collect taxes, arrest and execute people for the slightest resistance. Most of his fellow Party members are newly-arrived Russians or Russified Ukrainians. Though he heads the local Education Department, he must perform many other odious Party duties, often armed.

With a sharp eye for detail, the author has presented us with a whole gallery of Party workers, exploring their mentality and actions. Through Horobenko's eyes we see that the Party treats not only the villages as enemy targets, attacking and wreaking bloody havoc upon them. In the towns they confiscate private libraries and equipment which the Ukrainian intellectuals need to continue with their work.

And so throughout the book our hero, the upstanding Communist is forever duelling with his alter ego, the Ukrainian nationalist.

Dmytro Chub

DUEL

I

Kost Horobenko examined his Party ticket, and this time the familiar and rather ordinary words seemed to him much too expressive and ambiguous:

Russian Communist Party (Bolshevik).

A languorous thought occurred to Kost: what nonsense – to print the word 'Russian' in Ukrainian... And yet actually it wasn't this, which had caught his eye and continually drove him to pull the small pink book from his pocket when he was alone and to stare at the first page.

The whole essence of it, all of its durable force, which had focused his attention over the past few months, was to be found, it seemed, in that quite superfluous word tacked onto the end, hiding inside parentheses, but which in reality was neither superfluous nor ordinary – (Bolshevik)...

'Bolshevik!' This was by no means the same thing as 'communist'. 'Communist' was a new term, and Kost had grown accustomed to it straight away, even associating himself with it. But not with the word 'Bolshevik', that very same Bolshevik who, according to recent terminology had 'borne communism from the north of Russia to Ukraine' on the tips of bayonets – no.

Kost laid his Party ticket on the table and looked about the room. It was quiet. Through an open window came the monotonous twitter of some small ridiculous bird in the orchard. The sun was setting in the west, somewhere behind the leaves of the trees, and its pale rays painted a greyish marbled network on the wall. Books lay scattered about the room, there was a pair of pants on his pillow, a revolver on the table – all these things were deaf and dumb… Nothing here could eavesdrop on Kost's innermost thoughts, to voice them later in a hushed whisper to the organization's members in some corner behind his back. Kost calmly looked out the window into the orchard and said quietly to himself:

"I am a Bolshevik…"

He wanted to imprint this onto the very depths of his consciousness, but once more failed to do this. Kost became embarrassed and sat down, tired. A light ironical smile played on his lips. He felt uncomfortable. Just as he had once felt when he had deceived his parents by hiding his fail grade in dictation. Was there any difference here? Then it had been a fail grade, and now it was those two stores from which his luckless father had once traded in this very same town, and that high school which remained standing in a park on the corner of two streets, but in which they now held pedagogical courses. It was these things, which irritated his communist conscience or, more simply, his soul; it was this, which stopped him from calmly considering himself a Bolshevik, no different from all the other members of the organization. It was these things.

Kost rested his elbow on the table and thought: 'Why the hell is all this giving me no peace? Father was a petty bourgeois – that's true. It's a fact. What's more, he even kissed the hand of the synodal appointee, the auburn-haired Father Havrylo, and his sister, my aunt, was married a second time to a merchant who was a neophyte – this is true too. It's all true. But father took the trouble to die a year before the Revolution and, heaven preserve him, did well to do so. I detest him because he was my father and am grateful to him that he is no longer around. Now I have no one. All this is quite true. I am not responsible for my parents. And anyway: some were destined to be heirs of their class and others – renegades. Let it be, according to their theory, that I'm a petty-bourgeois intellectual! Although I see it a little differently – as a renegade of the petty bourgeoisie. It's more important how I see myself, than how someone else sees me. And I needn't reproach myself! Yes, I was a Ukrainian nationalist, I supported the head of the district branch of the National Alliance;[1] while still a moustacheless youth, fresh out of high school, I spoke at meetings in this town in 1917, crucifying myself at various gatherings in support of 'Mother Ukraine', calling as my witness the long-forgotten names of Cossack leaders such as Sirko and Hordiyenko. This is all fact and I'm not hiding it from anyone. But that's all in the past, and now I'm a...'

Kost paused again but strained and said aloud: "Bolshevik!"

Suddenly he recalled a folk tale from school or perhaps his childhood years, and it made him want to laugh and feel sad.

An alchemist had been seeking his philosopher's stone. He prayed to all the saints he knew, appealed to the Virgin Mary, and finally asked Christ Himself to help him, but all were silent, just like the ordinary stone of which his house was built. Then the alchemist cursed them all and turned to the devil. Satan eagerly agreed to help, but with one proviso: 'You'll find what you're seeking. There's only one condition, my friend: don't think of polar bears for a week'. The poor alchemist, who probably hadn't ever seriously thought about bears during his long life, let alone

---

[1]   Ukrainian National Alliance (*Natsional'nyi soiuz*) is an alliance of socialist parties opposed to Skoropadsky's monarchist Hetmanite government in Kyiv in 1918.

polar bears, could not think of anything else even for a moment the rest of that week.

Horobenko smiled and thought: 'Bolshevik – this is my polar bear, but what philosopher's stone am I seeking...?'

He replaced the Party card in his pocket, picked up his revolver, securely closed the window and left the house.

This detestable provincial town with its ridiculous dirty lanes, that shed in the marketplace, those awful pink merchant's houses, a town where everyone knew every trifle about one another and were thoroughly sick of each other – this town was witness to his past. It knew everything. Here was the public hall. His father had stood here with the tsar's portrait during a demonstration to mark the taking of Peremyshl; here was the marketplace and beyond it, to the left, the street where Nadia had lived with her aunt...

Kost strode quickly across the soft dust of the marketplace. The market was dead now. The half-destroyed stalls repugnantly projected their partly rotted rafters. They were the victims of the municipal department's struggle with private enterprise. The stalls stank of human excrement and the long row of meat stalls looked like collapsed horse skeletons.

In one corner several women were selling apples, squatting like accursed souls against the stone wall of a building; further on stood a peasant cart, and to one side of it was a wall with a sign cut in two by a downpipe:

Sapozhnaya masterskaya Uezdso/besa[2]

The downpipe had mercilessly split the two parts of the Russian word, making the first part '*Uezdso*' feel

---

2   Cobbler's Workshop of the District Social Security Office.

orphaned and lonely, however the '*besa*'[3] seemed quite appropriate. It had derisively jumped away from the downpipe and, pointing the tongue of its 'b' into the air, it laughed derisively at the pious townsfolk.

This led the women selling at the market, once wives of merchants and treasurers, to spread all kinds of uncertain rumours about the Antichrist (see, the authorities were also admitting that it was the devil's...).

An unexpected thought occurred to Horobenko: 'Had it been written in Ukrainian, this wouldn't have happened, even if the downpipe had split the sign in two.' However, he immediately became ashamed of his own primitivism. He had focused his attention on the wall not because of the '*besa*', but because the Petliurites had executed someone here. Horobenko smiled to himself:

'Actually, looking at it logically, given the climate of those days, I too should have been executed, and it's very strange that this never happened... True, I wasn't in the army, I was only involved in cheap politics, so to speak, but all the same...'

Horobenko crossed the wide paved main street and ascended the stairs of an entrance to a building. There had once been a bank here, where the father of a friend of his from the high school had worked, but now this was a workers club. Because of a lack of space in the District Party Committee offices, the organization's general meetings were usually held here.

Yellowed garlands of pine, paper flags and portraits of leaders hung sloppily on the walls, alongside posters sullied by flies and someone's dirty fingers, there was an untuned piano on which someone was forever hammering out The International – all this looked cold and

---

3   Genitive case of the Russian *bes*, meaning devil.

uninviting. There was no trace of a caring hand here and the place lacked spirit. People appeared here suddenly. They filled the hall with a noisy hubbub, bringing with them the smell of their skin, tar, grease, *makhorka*[4] tobacco, even the dust of country roads, and then chairs were scattered about, the floor became littered with cigarette butts and the room filled with a pall of thick bluish smoke. But when the people left, the room became quiet, empty, pervaded by sadness, and resembled a burnt-out ruin.

The general meeting had not yet begun. Party members were filing into the hall, drifting into corners in small groups.

Slavina rushed up to Horobenko. Her close-cropped hair did not suit her gaunt face, and he was quite annoyed by the ring on her finger.

"Comrade Garabyenko. Comrade Garabyenko." With her bony fingers she grabbed hold of his shirt button and began to twist it about mercilessly.

"Where have you been hiding? I really must talk to you."

Her Russian, with its fake Moscow accent, immediately fell several tones and lapsed into whispers. She gradually dragged Horobenko off into a far corner.

"You know… This is impossible…! This undermines our integrity. Firsov was drunk when he spoke at the teachers' meeting yesterday…! This must be included in the minutes without fail… If only you knew how he…"

Horobenko was looking for a way to get rid of her. This head of socialist education was really far too tiresome. He pushed his cap back and replied languidly:

"These are trifles, Comrade Slavina, now isn't the time to discuss them…"

---

4   A variety of strong tobacco commonly grown in villages.

But Slavina was already twirling the button with both her hands and whispered hastily: "What do you mean, trifles! This compromises us all... Such actions disgrace the whole Party... And do you know that this same Firsov..."

Horobenko looked impatiently into Slavina's eyes. He could see straight through this former teacher: she was seeking the support of the intelligentsia...

Once more he felt uncomfortable, for Slavina would never have gone to Horban or Druzhynin to whisper in their ears, instead she chose to direct her tirade at him. How repugnant this was! He looked at her thin bloodless lips and it suddenly occurred to him: 'Those rumours, that Slavina is the illegitimate daughter of some Tambov bishop, are probably quite true ...'

"Comrade Garabyenko! (Slavina stressed the name) We really must consider this together..."

Horobenko cut her short with his dry voice: "This is just a petty matter, comrade. Excuse me, I must go and talk to someone..."

Horobenko turned away sharply and went to join another group of people. Surprised, Slavina watched him leave, but immediately regained her composure and ran off to pester someone else...

Horobenko was stopped by Zavalny. As usual, the fellow grabbed hold of Horobenko's arms above the elbows and, testing his muscles, proceeded to shake him several times.

"Greetings, Horobenko. How's the 'language' going?"

Zavalny bared his teeth and the broad grin made his chin bristle.

"You're sowing the seeds of Petliurite nationalism, you dog! Tell me, was it you who Ukrainized Marx?" He pointed at the fresh posters printed in Ukrainian and flashed his front gold tooth.

These clumsy witticisms gushed in a torrent from Zavalny, but, despite the grin, Horobenko sensed a feeling of comradeship and goodwill in him. Zavalny was possibly the only fellow in the whole organization who read *The News*[5] and leafed through Shevchenko[6] at home.

Horobenko answered him in Russian.

"Listen, why the hell hasn't your Cultural Section organized a club library yet?" Popelnachenko piped up.

Popelnachenko was used to speaking in a peremptory, commanding voice, and this somehow inexplicably harmonized with his overly youthful facial features and lanky figure. He was still a boy, but he was the pet of the organization.

Popelnachenko thrust his chin into the air: "What do you mean there are no books! The intelligentsia has books – they must be requisitioned! Get in touch with the Board of Education. Just take them from the people and that's that!"

Popelnachenko could say such things. He had been in the Party since 1918. Popelnachenko had grown up being beaten with an iron ruler by his tailor father. He was a 'true proletarian'. As for the intelligentsia, that wasn't a random comment. He understood everything, this bandy-legged Popynaka, as he was nicknamed in the organization. He was a cunning one and knew where to throw his punches.

And yet he suffered from consumption. It had probably filled Popynaka's whole being with malice, weighing down the corners of his puffy lips. Why then was Popynaka loved in the organization? For loved he was! Popynaka could get away with blue murder.

---

5   The News (*Visti VUTsVK*), was the largest circulation Soviet Ukrainian newspaper of the day, founded in Kharkiv, 1918.

6   Taras Shevchenko (1814-1861), Ukraine's most popular poet.

Popelnachenko slid his hands deep into his trouser pockets and contemptuously screwed up his eyes with their long black eyelashes: "You, brother, I'm telling you Horobenko, you're a genuine one-hundred-percent intellectual. You should be sent off three times or so to deal with the kulak rubbish – then you'd be hardened, but the way you are now…"

Popynaka didn't finish. He choked in a fit of coughing, which resounded loudly throughout the room, bouncing off the ceiling, and left everyone feeling uncomfortable. People standing in groups nearby grew silent. A woman came running up with a rusty mug of water.

Popelnachenko waved his arms about and angrily spat to one side. Horobenko studied Popelnachenko's contorted figure and a thought drifted through his head like a wisp of cigarette smoke:

'He's a cynic all the same…'

At the table the Party Committee secretary, Krycheyev, yelled loudly: "Comrades, please take your seats! Please…"

He hammered his fists against the plywood and then said in a calm monotone, as if he was talking to someone in a corner of the room, rather than addressing a hall filled with Party members: "I propose we elect a chairman and a secretary…"

II

Horobenko sorted through a pile of stamped papers, hastily slipping them into folders, then stuffed some long sheets filled with writing into his briefcase, together with a piece of rationed oat bread, and left his Cultural Section an hour early.

The Party members had already assembled before the Party Committee offices and positioned themselves on the sidewalk in a clumsy mass of motley clothes, footwear and faces.

Slavina was unable to restrain herself this time either. Her uncovered close-cropped head atop a thin long neck was noticeable from afar. It was probably because of this thin, but agile neck, on which her head swivelled about in all directions from time to time, that Slavina resembled a bare-necked chicken. As if on purpose, Slavina wore a low-cut beet-coloured blouse, where Party decency duelled with Slavina's pretence for a décolleté. It was hard to tell which of them had won, however, the blouse accentuated her ugly neck and gave the impression of a chicken which had been plucked. With small chicken-like steps Slavina dashed in between the male figures and grabbed hold of Horobenko's briefcase. This immediately raised Horobenko's ire and brought to the surface the hostility lurking inside him. The devil knows, what a ridiculous habit she had, always needing to twirl something! Slavina kept fingering the glistening lock of his briefcase and ceaselessly scattered short words in every direction that her small head turned. This was not even speech, but a kind of staccato verbal stenography. From her thin lips emerged scraps of words with no beginning and no end: Slavina ground them up somewhere inside her narrow throat, and it was as if only the husks were being winnowed into the air, unpleasantly filling her interlocutor's ears with dust.

"It's a cinch to organize a kindergarten here… But first we need the parents… A meeting… We can consider the plan and hold a joint discussion… You're free on Friday… Then there's also the Husynka Library… Our candidate, Andriychenko, is ensconced there, but it's impossible. Her facial expressions, and then, you know, her behaviour… Generally speaking, our Women's Section…"

Slavina didn't finish. She grimaced, shook her head about and tugged deliriously at a corner of the briefcase.

"I don't know, I really don't know what all this will lead to… We need to think about it…"

However, Horobenko knew only too well that Slavina detested the Women's Section as a whole, and each female Party member in particular. She was principally against there being a Women's Section. The Women's Section in turn didn't like Slavina, and yet wanted to load her down with all the hard work, which Slavina avoided and shirked. Slavina took Horobenko aside a few steps and craned her neck over to his ear.

"And how do you like this? I have to be off to a meeting now, each of us is up to our ears with work, and here you go. Please. A *subotnyk*![7] This is out and out histrionics. Marching about the city… Fun – my oath…!" Horobenko looked in desperation at Slavina. She stuck to people like

---

7   A day of voluntary labour on community projects, usually on Saturdays.

a limpet. Indeed, she poisoned Party life for others. It was hard to get rid of her.

His tired gaze rested on her thin neck, and he suddenly thought:

'If only one could grab her neck in one's fist, this stalk of dough, and slowly squeeze it with one's fingers…!' He was even amused at the thought: Slavina would probably begin to scream, and would expire like one of those rubber devil puppets at the market…

Nearby a hoarse sergeant-major's voice barked:

"Fa-a-all i-in…"

This was the cavalry squadron commander, Nestorenko. He was appointed to take charge of the *subotnyk* and was all laced up with every needed and unneeded strap, his black field jacket inflated his well-built chest on the sidewalk.

The first to come out onto the pavement were the Party Committee secretary, Krycheyev, and the executive officials. They formed up in a line, and were followed by the grey Party masses who reluctantly left the sidewalk. This hasty execution of orders by Krycheyev and the executive officials seemed demonstrative and unnatural. 'Republican pseudo-simplicity!' Horobenko thought.

From the sidewalk the ever-present street urchins gawked, while the slightly startled townsfolk watched warily from their windows.

"…i-ick 'a-arch…!"

Up ahead the Party Committee flag with its golden star flapped wearily and a hundred boots marked time on the pavement.

Someone at the back of the line began singing in an uncertain, low voice, but the song was picked up by those in the middle ranks, and then the front rows joined in.

A semi-military, semi-youthful Russian song echoed through the streets:

> ...*Into the kingdom of free-eedom*
> *We'll carve a path with our chests...*

They sang in unison, but assiduously tried to compensate for their lack of vocal nuance with loud shouts of particularly significant words:

> ...*Long did they keep us in chains.*

The head of the Judicial Section, the flippant Mysha Chernyshov, was dissatisfied. He had long since supported the idea of organizing the Party members into a choir, but his idea had yet to gain support. He rejoiced wickedly, when someone broke off on a high note, or the singers sang out of key.

"Smarten up there! One-two, one-two..." Nestorenko half turned around and critically examined the undisciplined Party ranks.

"Druzhynin, stay in step!"

The lanky Druzhynin, who was marching alongside Horobenko, turned his head angrily in Nestorenko's direction and looked away. Without a word he fell in step and once again a weary shadow settled on his face under his leather cap, accompanied by a touch of reverie. Throwing her heels to the sides, Slavina stamped ahead of them. Nestorenko ran to the front of the column and his forceful voice rang out once more:

"Last on the right there, close up ranks...!"

Druzhynin spat to the side and swore. He placed his old, worn filer stuffed with papers under his arm and rolled a cigarette of *makhorka* tobacco, calmly puffing away on it.

Kost Horobenko studied his movements. This Druzhynin was one of the few who did not possess a briefcase. He stubbornly held onto his useless filer. Why? Slavina answered that question quite simply – because he was in charge of the Work Section. And who didn't know that lacklustre section...?

Kost Horobenko suddenly thought: which of them is the 'face' of our organization – Druzhynin or Nestorenko...?

The old *zemstvo*[8] tarantass rumbled past them, bearing the engineer and the contractor. They were the experts. The technical supervisors of this *subotnyk*. The engineer's pince-nez glistened as he ran his gaze over the Party ranks, but his Chekhovian face remained expressionless. He said something to his driver and lit up a cigarette further up the road.

Horobenko looked for a long time in the direction of the intermittent clatter of the tarantass.

What did this 'last of the Mohicans' think of them?

The street widened. They passed the last houses on the town's outskirts, but the merry crowd of urchins did not abandon the detachment. They ran on both sides of the street, catcalling, laughing, running right up to the ranks, and then scattering suddenly under Nestorenko's stern gaze.

Like tiresome flies, these boys teased Horobenko. In any case, Slavina was right: why this stupid display...? Couldn't everyone have assembled at an agreed place, without all this parading and singing? What use was that 'stay in step' and Nestorenko all decked out in straps? What the devil was all this farce for? To amuse the children and give the petty bourgeoisie an excuse to ridicule them...?

'Give the petty bourgeoisie an excuse to ridicule us?' Horobenko caught himself thinking and deliberately began to berate himself.

---

8   An elected council responsible for the local administration of a provincial district in tsarist Russia.

'You still care about the petty bourgeoisie, you care what they say?' he castigated himself. 'Own up – isn't it all the same to you? Or are you afraid of their jeering? Perhaps you want to justify yourself before them, eh? After all, everyone you associated with until recently, all of them were from the other side, all of them were petty bourgeois. Wasn't Nadia like that too? Didn't her merchant relatives still live in Moshchenka? What did they think of him, and how would Nadia herself have regarded all this, had she still been alive? Because Nadia was…!'

This began to resemble something more like self-torment, but there was something gratifying about it, something painfully pleasant, which swept clean his besmirched soul, like a guest room being spring-cleaned before a festive day. Hundreds of people, all quite different from one another, became a kind of solid, fused mass, so alien and distant to the whole provincial town with its old-fashioned merchant's houses.

He even felt overjoyed and light-hearted when the town ended, and they became swathed in the invigorating scent of pine trees.

The engineer and the contractor had long been standing near a pile of shovels beside several village carts, when the detachment arrived at the *subotnyk* site.

The engineer watched calmly over the top of his pince-nez, placed carelessly upon the middle of his nose, and said phlegmatically to Nestorenko:

"It's important to build up the abutment, the bridge itself will hold out. I'd ask you to split up into parties; one lot can dig the clay, and then, I guess, we'll also need…"

Horobenko scrutinized the engineer. He walked among the carts with Nestorenko and languorously gave instructions. He was no longer the mysterious sphinx that he had been in the tarantass. It was immediately evident that this 'specialist' considered all this work, this whole *subotnyk*, a complete waste of time. Under different circumstances the contractor and several labourers would have filled in the abutment, repaired the bridge, or might have even built a new one (the *zemstvo* would surely have allocated the necessary funds) – and everything would have been completed. The engineer would only have needed to inspect the finished job, he would have said a routine thing or two to the contractor, and in the evening would have settled down to a game of preference with the doctor and the magistrate. But now he had to cater to the whims of these grown children and to play the fool with them. For him, an old liberal, even a populist, this was difficult, it was moral torment, but there was nothing else he could do. This 'religious procession' had to be traversed. This was the fate of Russia's intelligentsia, which had broken free of its peasant roots. The path was painful and disgraceful, but its end would come. The engineer knew only too well that those who were against private enterprise would not be able to hold out for long! Trade was always the driving force behind progress and culture: take for example the Phoenicians, the Greeks, or the Romans… The engineer was sure of the future, but now he spoke courteously, though somewhat dryly and with restraint.

Horobenko pitied these hundred or so people of whom a good seventy believed in the *subotnyk* as a fetish of economic growth and were prepared to forget their undernourishment and exhaustion. The engineer's apathy contrasted with the forceful swing of everyone's arms. It seemed as if the engineer was sweeping soil from the shovels with his indifferent sceptical gaze through that horn-rimmed pince-nez, quashing the force of the blows, and turning this more into a child's game at workers. One wanted to throw the engineer the hell out of here, and with him his shadow – the contractor. Druzhynin spat into his palms, grabbed the shovel handle and, as if in answer to Horobenko's thoughts, growled:

"They've brought all kinds of bosses here! They need to plan. Tell me, please, what sort of a great deal is this! Can't we shovel this earth ourselves…?"

Meanwhile the engineer moved silently among the Party members and bored into their backs with his eyes. Horobenko dug deeply with his shovel, when he heard the engineer behind him tap a cigarette against his silver case and strike his lighter.

"Move away please, you're in my way!" Horobenko barked at him and forcefully tossed the shovelful of earth away.

The engineer looked around in surprise and, politely excusing himself, continued on his way. Horobenko said angrily in his direction:

"All kinds loafing about here…!" and briskly set to work.

It was already growing dark, but the results of the *subotnyk* were still quite paltry. The abutment was levelled out on one side only, while on the other side the earth lay unevenly in fresh clods and just before the bridge, where the rotting boards began, there was a large gaping black hole. It was obvious that even the essential things would not be completed that day, and the engineer was probably rejoicing already, but the Party members were keen to finish the work. Diligently they shovelled earth and brought it up to the bridge. Druzhynin deftly reinforced the slope, and only Nestorenko, District Supply Commissar Drobot and the organization instructor stood by the side of the road arguing about something.

Druzhynin removed his cap, wiped the sweat from his forehead with his sleeve, and rested on his shovel for a minute to catch his breath. He looked at Nestorenko's company and set to work again.

"No, first you reshape the man for me, that's what," he continued his diatribe with Zavalny, "because every man is scum in his own way. Understand?"

"Harping on the same string again, you 'god-seeker'?" Zavalny bared his teeth. "You philosophize too much, man!"

"I'll tell you straight, brother, that until you make a man out of each of our giddy Party members, a man, you understand, nothing will come of all this. Just look at them, brother," he nodded toward Nestorenko: "He can manage his 'hup-two!', but when it comes to pick and shovel work – excuse me! But I ask you, what the hell do we need an NCO for? Really...!"

Druzhynin swore and angrily waved his shovel about. Horobenko wanted to approach Druzhynin to talk with him. There was something amiable about his thin, hairless, deeply wrinkled face. Looking at Druzhynin's whiskers and beard one involuntarily recalled Ivanov's geography textbook: 'In the North the vegetation is more exiguous, with only patches of moss and lichen...' Druzhynin had a few yellowish hairs above his mouth and something wiry protruded from his chin in places, but what a kind face this Druzhynin had! His face beamed with something reminiscent of hard work and grief, something truly working-class, 'straight from the workbench'.

The head of the carpenters, Frolov, sat by the side of the ditch, his vest unbuttoned. He was sweating from the work he had done and lazily wiped the sweat from his bald patch with a muddy hand. His movements caused the thick silver-plated watch chain hanging from his vest to dangle heavily and tinkle with cheap trinkets. Stepping over shovels and fresh clods of earth, Mrs Frolov opulently walked past the scattered figures of the Party members.

"Semyon Petrovich, I've been looking for you everywhere. I barely managed to catch up to you all. Here, have a bite to eat…"

Mrs Frolov untied a small bundle of patties and laid them before her husband.

"My, it's so humid…! Why didn't you mention you had to go to a *subotnyk* today?"

Frolov rubbed the wet patches under his arms, feebly looked about him, and sighed. He was somewhat ashamed of the patties in front of the other hungry Party members and hesitated whether he should eat. Mrs Frolov understood his reluctance. She leaned over to her husband and whispered tenderly:

"That's all right, Senya. You take them, and then pretend you're going to relieve yourself in the rushes – you can eat them there.

Frolov grumbled angrily:

"All right, then. Go home. There's no need for you to be here…!"

Mrs Frolov hastened to her feet and whispered in parting:

"The darker ones are with meat, the others with cabbage…"

Slavina eyed Mrs Frolov askance and, seeing the patties, said with regret, as if to herself, but for everyone to hear:

"Amazing how stubbornly our comrades sometimes retain bourgeois habits…!"

Frolov did not hear her words. Still, he looked suspiciously at Slavina, drove his shovel into the ground and snuck off into the rushes.

It was already completely dark. A belated traveller's wheels were rattling across the road beyond the Vorskla River and a light mist hung over the water.

Slavina was standing beside Druzhynin, rearranging the small plait on her head. She was keen to pick an argument with someone.

"Undoubtedly, Comrade Zavalny. We must educate! Teach! And secondly, is this admissible: our 'rep' is terribly fond of smoked ribs (he makes entries in the protocol each day), and the likes of Comrade Nestorenko have three pairs of boots each – all this when we must sacrifice everything. We lunch in the Communist Dining Hall, we..."

Druzhynin wordlessly struck the abutment with his shovel.

Horobenko stopped work and stretched delightedly. An unusually pleasant, physical weariness spread through his body. The first stars lit up the night sky. Distant, fresh, dreamy stars. The same stars which had shone before the Revolution, during the Revolution, and which would shine forever after. Forever? Yes, yes – forever. There were many things, which were beautifully independent of everything. Would Druzhynin have been any the worse, had he not been a Party member?

Horobenko dismissed this sudden, tempting question and said to himself:

'No, it's very good that he's in the Party. He's a true, natural Party member."

Horobenko lay his shovel down and squatted on the spurge.

'Why the hell haven't they thrown Slavina out of the Party yet, though?'

From beyond the bridge came Nestorenko's booming voice: "Attention! Fall in, in two lines…!"

III

It was morning. The sun boldly cut through the green leafy mass with its golden swords, embroidering a fantastic tapestry on the wall. Kost Horobenko came up to the veranda parapet and took a deep breath of fresh air.

The morning was celebrating its triumph. Its azure forehead was not darkened by a single cloud. It had effortlessly tossed the night over the horizon and made its way victoriously toward day. Thousands of birds sang triumphal cantatas to it; the neglected dahlias, probably planted by the previous owners, and those common red irises in the orchard near the veranda seemed spruced up specially for today – washed, preened, a little saddened by their eternal silence, greeting the victor with gentle smiles.

And the morning marched on. Its invisible legions clad in golden armour rushed forward unchecked, and before their countless phalanges the last prince of night – the pale, barely visible moon – fled bent double across the heavenly expanses.

Horobenko leaned against a post grey with peeling paint and unbuttoned his collar. The morning freshness pleasantly penetrated his languid body, but the sunbeams had already overcome the last hurdles and burst through the damp leaves, their passionate breath trembling on Horobenko's chest. The sun inundated the veranda, and only a sorrowful piece of shade remained in one corner near the eaves, almost like a memory of someone's hopeless grief. Horobenko peered into this shade and found it dear to him. The intoxicating bliss of the sunshine and the lonely sorrow of the shade were related, they complemented one another like true brothers.

During the night Nadia had visited him in his dreams. The same Nadia who had once been, the Nadia who could now never be… Why?

Horobenko knew very well why, but he asked himself on purpose and answered frankly:

'Because back then she was simply Nadia, she was my fiancée (though this was never mentioned officially), but now she would have been a 'bourgeois', 'ballast', non-Party scum…'

Horobenko had said that on purpose. This crudeness contained a kind of sheer pleasure. But it was true. There was now no need to lie to the sun, the dahlias, or to himself. Maybe Nadia would have understood this too, had she been a reality, instead of a nice dream, but then… there was much beauty in things which were no more and could never be: in winter there would be no dahlias and no irises, but in one's memory they would be better than hothouse chrysanthemums; in a freezing gloomy snowstorm one easily recalled a clear, sunny spring morning… Nadia had died, she had died only physically, but when she occasionally appeared in his dreams, she would simply be Nadia, 'pre-Revolutionary' Nadia.

The janitor's wife, Paraska Fedotovna, came out onto the veranda with a trivet and a kettle. The Revolution had left its mark on her life first and foremost by the fact that the Housing Committee for the Poor had resettled her family from their kennel into a former aristocrat's study. She lived next door to Horobenko and was pleased with her quiet neighbour. Sometimes she even felt sorry for this taciturn 'commissar': 'He's a little queer: others have their own outlets, they celebrate 'communist' Easter secretly, in the old way, with roast pig, cheese *paska*[9] and alcohol, but this one…'

Paraska Fedotovna greeted him meekly, stood the trivet on the cement floor and floated off down the steps to collect some twigs in the orchard, returning to the veranda to light the fire. It was safer here: one could leave for a minute and no one would steal the kettle; besides, no one would see and pester her for some boiling water.

Horobenko looked at Paraska Fedotovna's plump figure and thought:

'It's strange: in all my time in the Party I haven't once been attracted to a woman. And it's not at all because of Nadia…'

When the lively fiery tongues began to jump about under the kettle, assiduously licking its dirty black bottom, Paraska Fedotovna wiped her hands on her skirt and turned to Horobenko:

"Warming yourself in the sun? It really is beautiful… Like a glass of tea? I'll just caramelize some sugar… 'Cause you know the sort of tea you get now …!" Paraska Fedotovna said with a sigh. "Before you could go down to the store and get Vysotsky's *Premium Quality* tea, and buy a lemon on the way at Pankratov's."

Paraska Fedotovna grumbled away exuberantly, and meanwhile the kettle began to boil over, and the fire hissed angrily from its first splashes.

"Please feel free to drop by and pour yourself a glass… it's all the same to me, but you, being a bachelor, how can you go off to work like that…?"

Paraska Fedotovna liked to chatter away like this to the strange 'commissar'; she wasn't even averse to flirting a little with him (this wasn't damned Mytka for you,

---

9   Easter cake.

who had beaten her for fifteen years when he was drunk, but was now unable to satisfy the old wench's appetite). Paraska Fedotovna winked slyly at Horobenko and went back inside the house.

Horobenko returned to his room, took off his shirt and began to wash himself. Splashing in all directions, he threw cold water onto his neck and chest, and whether it was because of the water or his movements – his pensiveness vanished without a trace and his body filled with energy and vigour. Drying himself with a coarse towel, Horobenko paused for a moment to look at his fairly well-developed muscles, and for some reason suddenly thought: 'It'll be a pity, anyway, when I'm killed, and this supple healthy body turns into abhorrent crackling.'

Horobenko ate a slice of stale oat bread with some oil but didn't drop by Paraska Fedotovna's for a cup of tea.

The sun was already quite high, and it was becoming humid outside when Horobenko emerged from his alley into the wide street, which led straight to the trade-union Cultural Section. There were already quite a few people heading in the opposite direction: this was the time when people returned from the market. Horobenko spied plump Mrs Frolov, loaded down with a heavy basket. This was the wife of the head of the carpenters. A chicken head and carrot tops protruded from her basket. Mrs Frolov moved along luxuriously, pleased with herself.

Horobenko felt bad. How ridiculous this was: they fought against markets, and at the same time the wives of communists went there to buy things, and hadn't even he himself gone there to buy some *makhorka* tobacco? And others went too. The collective farm had demolished the meat stalls, so now the butchers lay the meat out straight on the ground. What was better? The day before the militia had dispersed the market, and now the produce had tripled in price...

But the market survived, just as it had been before the Revolution, becoming even livelier and more colourful. It was the final hope and joy for many. What would Mrs Frolov be left with if the market really did disappear?

Frolov's wife had already opened their gate and entered her yard, but at that moment her shrill, irate voice rang out:

"How many times have I told you not to draw water from our well! I don't know, what the hell you think this is...!"

A red-haired fellow barked back from the well in the yard and quickly made his way into the street with a full bucket.

"...May you choke on your well! My, what a clucky housewife...!"

"I don't want to see this happening again! You think my husband will be fixing everything up after you...? We dug this well. You can dig as many as you like for yourself..."

Frolov's wife hastened to the well and, seeing a fresh puddle near the well joists, shook her head angrily.

"May you all croak...!"

Frolov himself emerged from the orchard, dressed only in his vest. He ran his hand guiltily through his short hair and said to his wife:

"I told you – we need to tie a dog to the well. Otherwise you'll never stop this..."

Druzhynin stood on the street corner and chatted with the red-haired fellow, who was holding the bucket of water and waving his free arm about, pointing with his finger in the direction of the Frolovs' yard.

Horobenko greeted them and quickened his step. Behind him he heard Druzhynin's quiet words:

"I'll bring it up at the Party committee meeting... There is scum everywhere, but this can't be rectified straight away..."

In the doorway of the trade-union building Horobenko was stopped by the Party committee clerk, Holtsev.

"Want to see something interesting?" Holtsev brought his long hooked nose to his ear, and screwing up an eye, said softly: "It's about you..."

Horobenko looked questioningly into Holtsev's colourless eye, which was peering craftily from under red eyebrows. Forcing a smile, the fellow hastened to explain:

"Your character reference from the Party committee to the *gubernia*. Let's step into your office." He lightly nudged Horobenko and they made their way to the second storey of the former spacious home of some merchant. What did Holtsev actually want? And why these visits of his, and that conversation about his supposed former job as a printer for the Directory's[10] Ministry of Land Affairs, and all this somewhat unnatural friendliness. Horobenko looked askance at Holtsev's grimy merchant's pants and suddenly thought: 'He's a secret agent! Been charged with watching me...' He felt disgusted but was surprised: 'To operate so openly! They could have used someone else... Couldn't they find someone more respectable...?'

Horobenko sat at his desk, unlocked the drawers and looked sharply at Holtsev... A peculiar cunning smile played on the fellow's face. Short wrinkles spread like thorns from the corners of his eyes, and his large greasy lower lip protruded slightly forward. It seemed as if Holtsev had

---

10   The Directory of the Ukrainian National Republic – a revolutionary government, which succeeded the monarchist Skoropadsky regime in late 1918.

already manufactured this smile long ago, working out its every detail, and when needed he could slap it onto his face in a flash like a mask, removing it just as quickly. Holtsev waited a minute in silence, then bent over his briefcase and swiftly rummaged through his papers. Pulling out a sheet of bluish sugar paper, he grabbed the chair and moved closer to Horobenko. Screwing up one eye again and nudging Horobenko with his sharp elbow, he whispered quietly:

"Only, please, this is just between us… You must realize, of course, that this character reference is secret… But I thought to myself, why shouldn't I let a friend of mine like Horobenko know…" With his long thin hand covered in black hairs Holtsev made an uncertain gesture and slapped the smile back on his face.

There was something repugnant in this intimacy, in his drawing up a chair and those unceremonious nudges. Horobenko moved away involuntarily and wanted to refuse point-blank to read the Party committee's character reference, but looking at Holtsev, he immediately became confused. Holtsev's smile seemed to paralyze his movements, settling upon his head in a dense mass.

"Here…" Holtsev moved the sheet of paper over to him. Still stunned, Horobenko looked at the careless, scattered lines and greedily ran his eyes over the form, as if it were something illicit.

There wasn't much there, but it was quite clear:

'As a Communist-Bolshevik (someone seemed to have underlined this second word almost deliberately and consciously) – he is unstable, on account of his previous membership in Ukrainian organizations), but as a cultural worker he can be used on the provincial level.'

With a certain effort Horobenko tore his eyes from the form and reddened a little. He was watched by Holtsev's silent lifeless smile.

IV

The hasty patter of Holtsev's feet on the wooden steps had long since gone cold and disappeared, the typewriters had already been clattering away for an hour, clattering monotonously and far too tediously, but Horobenko remained sitting at his desk without making a move. A drawer full of folders, a stamp, piles of paper and a packet of cheap tobacco remained half-opened after Holtsev's departure. It was like a tentacle about to grab his very soul, dragging it into the yellow, ink-stained, scratched and pockmarked monstrosity of the old office desk with its torn green material.

Horobenko could not collect his thoughts for a long time. They flitted away in every direction like sparrows and all he saw before him were the words, 'as a Communist-Bolshevik – he is unstable', and Holtsev's screwed-up eye.

Horobenko lowered his hands, squeezed his interlocked fingers together till they cracked, and thought: 'This is probably Popelnachenko's doing...' But immediately he looked askance at his briefcase and decided: 'Isn't it all the same, after all! The important thing is that it has been stated, that someone has definitively and clearly enunciated the things which I was unable to say to myself.'

And yet it was unpleasant and painful. And once more those two buildings once owned by his father surfaced in his mind, and that Prosvita[11] organization, and the year

---

11   Literally means "enlightenment". A cultural and educational

1917… Horobenko became annoyed. 'Unstable'…? Could he ever be stable to them? Could they ever forget his past? They were like monks who in their frenzied fanaticism could never forgive him this, never – not until he lay in his grave. And then this Ukrainian thing, what was it to them? They, for whom there was no Solonytsia, nor Berestechko, nor Poltava, nor even Kruty![12] For whom history was just an eternal class struggle… Oh, how dogmatic they were…!

Horobenko ran his hand over his forehead and his eyes rested on Trotsky's pince-nez. As familiar and just as irksome as any portrait, which existed in this world, the portrait seemed quite different to Horobenko now. It had assumed new features, and these features said a lot. An energetic beard, two deep wrinkles from the nose to the corners of the mouth and a serene, hard, distant gaze. The eyes were barely visible because of the pince-nez, and yet the gaze remained. People with such gazes saw far beyond the present day. They never experienced hesitation, they had no damned beating about the bush to worry about, and their prospects were plain as day. They had their eternal formula: 'Existence determines consciousness…' This was their verity, this was the 'new testament' with which they would take the world, reploughing the whole earth, erasing all borders, mixing all nations into a single torrent, a black mass of trampled slaves, which had broken its banks. Marx's *Das Kapital*… What was this? A Torah, a Bible, an Al-Koran or an Archimedean lever…? They were so strong, these people in pince-nez with distant gazes and the fanaticism of Islam!

---

community organization existing in Ukraine from the mid 1800s to the late 1930s.

12   All were battles in which the Ukrainian forces were defeated.

Horobenko sat hunched up in his armchair, but it seemed that he wasn't sitting at all, that he was just hanging onto a tiny bit of it, on the very edge near the armrest. The inkstand on the desk was more firmly planted than he in his armchair, even the penholder and nib beside the inkstand had more support than him. Everything around him, to the smallest trifle, was far too distinct, there was only a crushed intimacy sitting inside him. It had become so deeply entrenched inside him, that he seemed to feel his own skin, even the hair on it in some parts, and here there was a protruding finger. Was it his or someone else's…?

Horobenko stole another glance at the portrait, and then someone's mighty hand seemed to stroke his head, and everything became quite clear:

'They're right… What are you? Perhaps it's only idle chatter, that 'history is the struggle of classes'? No. They are still quite restrained. They are simply curiously soft toward you. You are unquestionably 'unstable'. Yes, yes. And why? Because of whom and what? Because of your ancestors, who gave birth to Kochubeys, Halahans and Yuzefovyches[13] or because of those kitsch Prosvita members, or is it simply because of the cherry orchards, the stars, the darling flowers and that tinsel called 'national separatism'?'

Ah, how ridiculous this was, that a nation could stand between him and the Party. A nation, which had invented only the *bandura* and the *plakhta*![14] This really was nonsense. An anecdote.

The door burst open and the room filled with the

---

13   Ukrainian traitors. Kochubey betrayed Mazepa to the Russian tsar, Halahan helped the tsarist army destroy the Zaporozhian Cossack fortress, and Yuzefovych was the author of the Ems Ukase, which forbade the use of the Ukrainian language in 1876.

14   The bandura is a Ukrainian folk string instrument. The *plakhta*

chatter of wooden sandals. The Party committee courier opened his folder without saying a word, rummaged about in the papers and handed Horobenko a notice.

"They requested you come as soon as possible."

Something creaked across the floor, there was a thud, and then a clatter down the passage. Horobenko watched the courier's grey shirt disappearing through the door and then read: 'Upon receiving this note, please come immediately to the district Party committee office.' It was an ordinary, perhaps even hackneyed note, however he immediately became worried for some reason. Perhaps he was afraid? No, no. He just felt a little uncomfortable, for there was some matter requiring his presence. His alone. From among the whole Party collective Horobenko was to become quite distinct for a while, placed under the microscope, so to speak; he had to present himself before the intelligent, but sharp eyes of Secretary Krycheyev and the Party leadership. This meant having to be internally at attention, knowing that Krycheyev's glasses were boring deeply into him, looking specifically at him. In any case, the very existence of this Party committee notice signified that there was another reason. What was it? Good or bad? However, one shouldn't expect good news from the Party committee.

Horobenko hurried off to the Party committee office. Only those who wanted to learn about a misfortune so that they could be rid of it as soon as possible moved with such haste.

Here were the worn steps, the iron handrails of the former hotel, the passage, the posters, the offices of the organizational instructor and political propaganda section, another door, two fellows with rifles perched on

is an ancient waistline garment composed of two widths of woollen cloth sewn partly together and worn instead of a skirt.

the windowsill, husking sunflower seeds, and the door to Krycheyev's office. For the briefest of instants, which would not have registered on a watch but could only be perceived in one's mind, Horobenko paused at the door. Then he hastily pulled on the handle, yanked at it sharply more likely, and entered.

Krycheyev and Popelnachenko were hunched over a sheet of paper with tiny writing. Krycheyev didn't look up straight away, but when he did, he said casually: "Wait a minute," and returned to running his dry pen over the lines.

Horobenko came up to the desk with weary steps. He leaned on the desk with his hand, but then moved his hand away and pushed his cap back. Only now did he feel how tired he was. It was stuffy, he could hear his heart racing away under his shirt from all the walking and the stairs, and there was nowhere to rest his eyes on the endless monotone diagrams and portraits, which covered the grey walls here and there. The portraits and diagrams seemed to highlight his fatigue. He was quite exhausted. Maybe one could become tired by simply living? Of course, one could. Then what was relaxation for…? But…

Horobenko pulled back, quickly moved away from the desk and sat down on the nearest chair. 'Why didn't I sit down straight away? Well, that's obvious: I was standing before the secretary – my superior. Whoever said: 'There is something subservient in the psyche of every Ukrainian,' was right.'

Popelnachenko rose to his feet, while Krycheyev turned to Horobenko:

"This is what it's about, comrade. A group of the local Ukrainian intelligentsia has submitted a request to allow them to publish a non-Party journal. In Ukrainian, of course. Their deposition is over there..."

Horobenko moved his chair closer to the table.

"You must of course realize that we're not quite competent in such matters. Therefore – your thoughts, as a Ukrainian?"

Popelnachenko lit a cigarette and slid his thin, bony hands into the pockets of his yellow chrome leather coat. Krycheyev moved the papers to one side, adjusted the pince-nez on the bridge of his nose and threw his head back against the armchair.

"Here then. We'd like your opinion."

Horobenko looked at Krycheyev's pince-nez and for some reason picked up the hole punch off the desk. He turned it around three times by the handle and replaced it in its place. And then it became hilariously obvious: they were listening. Great. But this was far too naive. Just too much. Could they really think that he did not realize what this was leading to. They simply wanted to make sure once more how true the statement on the form was: 'As a Communist-Bolshevik – he is unstable!' All right.

Kost Horobenko screwed up his forehead, folded his arms, and said calmly:

"In my opinion the request should be unequivocally refused."

Krycheyev raised his eyebrows, as if in surprise, and asked again:

"So, you think it should be refused?"

"Definitely. Because any such journal would in fact be…"

Popelnachenko sarcastically slanted his pale lips and interjected:

"As for me – I'd let them go ahead. Let them print it."

Popelnachenko strode over to Horobenko and slapped him chummily on the shoulder:

"By God, you're an odd one, Horobenko! It's signed by all those fellows who used to be in Prosvita, remember:

Kovhaniuk, Prydorozhny, that long-haired agronomist, what's his name, Pedashenko or something? You have to support them! What the devil…"

Horobenko blushed, turned the hole punch around one more time, but facing Krycheyev, said firmly:

"If anyone wants to support legalized Petliurite nationalism – it's up to you. Personally, I abstain."

Cunningly screwing up his eyes, Popelnachenko looked at Horobenko and smiled. Krycheyev nodded his head as a sign that the official business was over and bent over his papers once more.

"We'll take your thoughts into consideration, Comrade Horobenko. You are probably right."

Krycheyev turned over a page and picked up a pen.

His last words seemed like a dull echo of praise or simply justification, however Horobenko cut short all his feelings and sharply made for the door.

"All the best…!"

Resting his knee on a chair, Popelnachenko mockingly watched him leave.

V

A small lamp flickered away on the chair beside the bed, however it was impossible to read by its light. Kost Horobenko dropped the newspaper onto the floor and rubbed his strained red eyes. The whole room was filled with an orphan-like ribbon of light – a miserable flame from the night-lamp – and the thick hairy silence seemed to hold its countless black hands together, pressing tightly around the flame. On the darkened, smoke-stained ceiling clung the neglected shadow of the chair and the door glistened dully.

Horobenko turned over on the bed toward the night-lamp and adjusted the soiled pillow under his head. The lamp burned away quietly. Occasionally its flame would swing unexpectedly to one side, becoming nervous, beginning to dawdle, but then calmed down again. Horobenko looked at it and the small flame melted away the secretiveness and wariness he had fostered while in the Party, casting unexpected thoughts, peering into his very soul and provoking frankness.

Paraska Fedotovna suddenly cried out on the other side of the wall, and then he heard the hoarse drunken booming of her Mytka.

"Devil, Satan, communist, anarchist – it's all the same! They've spun a fine one: revcom, prodcom, Soviet, but action there's none. Understand: there used to be a Russia, what a Russia! And now it's tiny, very tiny. And I ask you, why? Tell me – why?!"

Paraska Fedotovna swore and burst into tears, wailing in a long howl. Then there was the clatter of a falling stool as Mytka probably tried to stand up, and then the crash of broken glass on the floor. He heard the sound of rustling and the rabid screams of Paraska Fedotovna.

Over these past few months Horobenko had grown used to these scenes. The clatter and shouts passed through the wall, entered his ears, but proceeded no further. The night-lamp only served to heighten Horobenko's solitude and lit up a hidden corner in the endless corridors of his soul. The events of the last few days surfaced, together with that audience the day before yesterday at the Party committee office, and Popelnachenko's sarcastic smile. Horobenko stirred, as if someone had placed something cold against his bare skin, and his chest ached with indignation. He felt even more hurt now, than at the time. He really had to do something. He had to put a decisive end to this. Just to think that some Popelnachenko, a mere kid, could actually allow himself such jokes! It was simple mockery! What did it matter that he had been in Prosvita and that all these Kovhaniuks and Pedashenkos were seeking a legal means to vegetate? He wanted to spit on them all…!

Horobenko rolled over onto his back and put his hands under his head. And at that moment a treacherous recollection surfaced. This same Kovhaniuk had risked his own life by harbouring Horobenko in his home when Denikin's men had been searching for him. And together with Pedashenko they had organized a branch of the National Alliance and arrested the district hetmanite village elder. And with Prydorozhny…

These annoying recollections were like drops of mercury, grabbing onto each other and growing into a large ball which drew closer and closer, crowding out the present day, painting the year before last in far too fantastic and admittedly beautiful, pleasant, dear pictures, making him hurt inside even more.

"Conscience…? Hah?"

Horobenko threw off the blanket and lowered his feet to the floor. For a minute or so he listened to the hubbub of inner voices, watched closely their struggle and… was even amazed.

Quietly, hedging about, a long familiar thought emerged from the nooks of his subconsciousness. Well yes: he had decided this a long time ago, only until now he wasn't able to voice it out loud:

'They must be killed… I must execute them, rather than kill them. And then, when their blood appears before my eyes, when this blood of executed rebels, kulaks, speculators, hostages and countless other categories which all have one common denominator – counterrevolution – when it falls at least once on my head, as they say, soiling my hands, then all this will come to an end. Then the Rubicon will have been crossed. Then I will be liberated. Then I can tell myself boldly and openly, without the slightest hesitation and doubt: I am a Bolshevik.' With trembling hands Horobenko hastily rolled a cigarette and paced about the room. An enormous curved shadow appeared on the wall and the silence and darkness gave way to the steps of bare feet. Horobenko greedily inhaled the first stream of smoke, and suddenly the room seemed to become lighter. The flame of the lamp jumped about in a frenzy, its yellow string seemed as if it would be cut at any moment, however the thought remained firmly entrenched in his mind and, like a mole, burrowed deeper.

'Yes, yes – a few drops of blood must fall on the ground. Only they will wash everything away. Then everything will be permissible, and I can spit on everything. Just once! There in the village, among those traditional orchards and white houses, all those various "lovely flowers", in overalls and dust mixed with sweat, with soiled hands – I must execute them… It is important to do it at least once. And no less a man (and this is important) than an insurgent. Yes. That same stubborn peasant, who in the twilight of a Poltava grove has dreamed up an "independent" Ukraine and pulled on a red pointed beret over his dishevelled dirty hair!'

Horobenko had been pacing about the room from corner to corner for a long time. Everything, which had previously been an incomprehensible obstacle had now become quite clear, almost planned out. Now he understood what had previously stopped him. Now there would be no wavering. Now he would simply have to make his way toward his goal. What had been born now, had to be brought to fruition, for it was constantly growing and demanded an outlet. Horobenko stopped in the middle of the room. It was stuffy. He went over to open the window and saw that dawn was already breaking outside. Through the serene branches of the trees he could see the grey blanket of sky. Horobenko opened the window with a rumble, and the first twitter of a bird drifted into the room. In the corner by the bed the alien, now unnecessary lamp was burning low. Horobenko extinguished it and calmly went to sleep.

VI

Kost Horobenko requisitioned all week long.

He dashed into the Board of Education nearly every morning for the warrants, ran across the road to the Department of Labour to pick up a mobilized cart and several porters and then the operation itself began. The large awkward cart, which had previously carried flour, would stop unexpectedly before someone's front entrance. White from flour and chalk, the porters lazily got down from the cart and made themselves comfortable on the steps for a smoke, while Horobenko came up to the door and knocked energetically three times.

A minute or two later the door was carefully opened by a worried owner's hand, and Horobenko decisively crossed the threshold and handed over the warrant.

"I need to requisition your piano. Please show me where it is…"

The owner's hands irresolutely took the order and, without reading it, the eyes stared dully at the smudged stamp and timidly crossed to Horobenko's face, the feet hesitating whether to make a move.

Holding his mouth tightly closed, Horobenko stared into the owner's eyes for a while, and then, shuffling from foot to foot, announced coldly:

"I've no time to waste. People are waiting outside. Please, don't hold us up."

He turned his head toward the street and shouted loudly:

"All right, comrades, ready there."

Waddling along on their strong legs, the porters entered the room phlegmatically, as if they were coming into a storeroom, went into the rooms and filled them with an unusual din. Without waiting for the owner's reply, Horobenko strode off ahead of the porters into the house, rummaging about the rooms with his eyes as he sought the piano.

Then the owner's figure came to its senses, seeming to recover its gift of speech and, stuttering, it fearfully began the usual verbal procrastination:

"Actually, this piano… You see, we don't have it for entertainment… My daughter is learning to play, she has a good ear… I myself work in the statbureau… I beg you, comrade, couldn't we somehow…"

These eternal dramatic preludes frightfully irritated Horobenko. He hurriedly broke off the owner in mid-sentence:

"Read the warrant? It's settled. What's there to talk about!"

He rushed up to the piano first, clearing the way of chairs, coffee tables and armchairs, removed portraits and books from the piano as if he were at home, and moved the piano from its place, where it had rested all these long serene years.

The room became filled with the faces of frightened, desperate members of the owner's family, but Horobenko tried not to look at them.

"All right, comrade, give me a hand… come in from the right there… Come on – together! Once more… Slower, slower! Careful…"

Horobenko heard a girl's fingers crack, wrung in helpless grief, sensed that the owner's lips attempted to utter something and yet did not dare, and meanwhile he helped the porters shift the piano from the room intently and assiduously, as if there was no one else in the place apart from them. The piano left its place unwillingly, humming angrily, bumping into chairs, the doorpost, as if pleading with them to hold it back, not to let it leave the house, and over its hollow funereal boom the air behind him was cut by the involuntary rolling sobs of a woman crying, uttering feeble entreaties and muffled curses.

Prudently shifting aside furniture from the path of the porters, the owner's figure rushed ahead to open the front door properly, so the piano wouldn't be scratched and asked Horobenko something on the run. The owner's bowed legs and hunched back could not believe that the piano was being removed for good, he tried to convince himself that it was only being moved from place to place for some reason, that it would suffice to utter some magical word and everything would be settled, everything would return to normal. But the owner's lips could not find the right word. Very harsh, it swirled about in his head, unable to crystalize into a concrete form. For this reason, the trembling lips mumbled some vague absurdity, and the arms fluttered about to help these dirty clumsy visitors, if need be.

When the piano was being stowed on the cart and tied down with ropes, Horobenko usually turned to face the front door and, without looking anyone in the face, called out in a bloodless voice:

"If you have any complaints, you can contact the Board of Education or the RKI[15]…"

Then he said loudly to the carter:

"Let's go! Only take it easy there on the rocks," and he left.

---

15   Acronym for Worker-Peasant Inspection – an organ of state control.

BORYS ANTONENKO-DAVYDOVYCH

He returned to his permanent job in the trade union office with a sure, firm step, but along the way he pictured the stupid, disconcerted physiognomy of the owner, the red tear-stained face of the daughter, the jabbering of the stout *mamasha*...

He tried to imagine in great detail the atmosphere in the house orphaned of its piano, painted the despair and grief of the people he had just left – and this gave him a kind of wicked satisfaction. He remembered those families who still somehow managed to have pianos and grand pianos and planned further requisitions. He not only made use of the Board of Education's warrants but pushed for new requisitions too. Through various means he obtained lists of registered and unregistered pianos, also raising the question of the requisition of private book collections, and loaded carts creaked toward the centre of town for a whole week. Beautiful oak desks, books in expensive bindings, cupboards, black doleful pianos – all this was removed from imposing studies, cosy lounge rooms, and rattled away over the damaged pavement to some building with bare, pockmarked walls, inside which an invisible spider spun a dirty web of mute emptiness.

The pianos were transported immediately according to assignation – to the club, children's home and schools – one concert grand piano somehow found its way into the library. Writing desks and cupboards also found refuge in various offices, departments, and sections. But it was far worse with the books. They were unsystematically dumped on the floor of an empty room in the public hall and here, on the dirty boards, countless titles from various fields of knowledge, science and art found a long resting place. In thick layers they spread the breadth and length of the room, the lower layers becoming covered in decaying dust, while new layers continued to rise above them.

And thus, day by day, the room became more and more like an uncovered common grave.

In these four walls with their large dirty stains from the damp, the serenity banished from life was buried with the books. Smells innate to individual families and people, the monotony and unconcern of district homes where people read *The Southern Land* beside the samovar, subscribed to *Niva* and respected both Pushkin and Gogol, the desiccated thoughts (just like a herbarium collection) of demure studies, Maupassant's delicacies belonging to former high-school girls – all this had been picked up by the flood, after the dams and weirs were broken one stormy night, and had been washed up here.

It seemed everyone had lost faith in books. None of the Party members or the plebeians ever came here, no one leafed through the books. More than half of them could have been pilfered, taken home in sacks, but no one was willing.

Even the library officials, despite an order, came only once and took a few books for appearances sake.

Only Kost Horobenko entered this room, sitting among the paper cadavers like an undertaker for hours on end.

Like the estate of a former landlord, these books fascinated Horobenko. When he entered here, he first cautiously listened by the door to see if anyone was following him, then slowly closed the door, locked it, and then waded into the thick of the books. He picked up individual volumes, enormously thick bound collections of journals, and leafed through them. Occasionally he would stop at some chance page, which had suddenly caught his attention for some unknown reason and began to read. He read for a long time, as if by inertia, his eyes passing over page after page, until the twilight thickened in the room and his eyes became tired. Then he moved aside what he had read and looked at magazine illustrations.

Recollections floated from the old, yellowed pages of *Homeland*, *Around the World* and *Niva*, stained here and there with coffee, all so familiar in his childhood. They were associated with countless days, so snug and fragrant. These magazines were like a diary. Naive, a little foolish, but so simple, so close, so dear, like all that which had been, and which would never, never return. His deceased father had looked at these same pictures, so had his mother, who was still alive somewhere, and he had looked at them too. Looked at them when the swing of life was measured by the high-school timetable, when life ran along confidently, untroubled and joyous, like a sled after the first snow...

Horobenko looked through the magazines until it was quite late, and amid the dust of the books, quietly, without remorse, without self-reproach, his childhood memories festered.

As he left the room one evening, he remembered with horror that sooner or later the books would disappear. The time would come, and they would be dragged off to libraries, given away to schools or pilfered – would anything survive this 'general ruin', this gigantic invisible plough stubbornly ploughing over the last vestiges of the past...?

And he grieved over the books. They were the last 'material evidence', which had been carried like splinters through the froth, the rocks, ledges and waves of the rapids of the revolution. They alone could secretly tell so much inside the four walls of this sullen, damp room! They alone...

Subconsciously Horobenko wanted to hold onto these books in the public hall for as long as possible. He reminded no one of them, diligently bringing more and more new tomes to this pagan temple.

The day before yesterday he had hung his own lock on the door, as well as propping the door up with a bench today.

VII

It was already growing dark when Horobenko returned home. He quickly removed his dirty boots, hurled them into a corner, and was about to stretch out on his bed when there was a knock at the door.

"Come in. Who's there?"

The door was quietly opened by Paraska Fedotovna and someone's grey head appeared behind her from the evening twilight.

"Someone here to see you," and she again disappeared behind the door to allow the grey head to enter the room. "Please, he's at home…"

Kost Horobenko threw on his field jacket and stepped toward the door.

"May I? Thank you… Allow me, Konstiantyn Petrovych, I have a request… Recognize me? I've come to see you about a certain matter…"

Kost didn't recognize him straight away. With his grey shaggy hair, one cheek bandaged with a handkerchief, and, finally, all hunched forward, much too shabby, almost like a beggar – there was no way he could have recognized him.

Kost moved a stool up for him and stole a look into his face.

"Sit down, please."

"Thank you, thank you…" His back bent even more and it looked as if his arms would fall off at any moment, his head would roll away somewhere, and his feet dawdled fearfully in one spot when he plonked down on the stool, working his old coat under himself. "I've become ill, you know: the teeth and liver... Excuse me, Konstiantyn Petrovych, for..."

Horobenko became suspiciously wary. Why had this former merchant, the brother of that convert of a merchant who kept his blood aunt, come to see him? He was a convert too, and obviously just as much a scumbag.

"Well then, Konstiantyn Petrovych, there's one small matter here, but..."

Horobenko was unpleasantly surprised by this respectful use of patronymic. Earlier, when he had been a high school student, he had met this fellow only once a year at his aunt's name-day parties; this merchant would exchange two or three words with him out of sheer kindness, calling him only 'Kostyk'. Now he was wheedling for something... And Horobenko became even more wary. With concealed disgust he looked at the tattered coat, quite unnecessary in summer, at the fellow's contorted fingers, and said dryly:

"Please, I'm listening."

"You still speak Ukrainian... I remember once when you recited Shevchenko at Varvara Mykolayivna's... *The Rapids Roar*, or something like that... Heh-heh..." The old man laughed prudently with a false petty chuckle, which made Horobenko quite angry. An end had to be put to this family familiarity and all these reminiscences. He sharply interrupted the chuckling.

"Forget about all that. And Varvara Mykolayivna has nothing to do with this. What is it you want from me?"

Horobenko buried his spread-out fingers in his hair and looked the old man straight in the face. But the old fellow kept procrastinating. Using every means at his disposal, he tried to delay that most important thing which

60

BORYS ANTONENKO-DAVYDOVYCH

had brought him here to the place of this accursed Bolshevik, who had once been an ordinary meek high-school student.

The old man wanted to do some verbal spadework, to soften the communist's leather heart, to display all the patches of his bountiful life, to prove that he was no longer a merchant, but a proletarian like everyone else, trying to play on family strings; other commissars helped their relatives evade all kinds of requisitions and the installation of new tenants. The old man fearfully swallowed the last warble of his chuckle and wriggled about on the stool. Then with guilt and humiliation, like a dog before the sting of its master's whip, he stretched a gentle smile across his wrinkled face:

"Forgive me, forgive me, Konstiantyn Petrovych... It just somehow happened to slip out – the past came to mind, you know. It all seems so recent... your auntie, your father..."

Horobenko's raspy impatient voice sounded from the table near the window:

"I haven't time to listen to you for too long, so get to the point."

The old fellow became completely confused and in despair suddenly proceeded to the purpose of his visit, without beating about the bush anymore and making allusions.

Bending over the table, Horobenko impatiently watched the bandaged cheek from over his hand. The old man was already gesticulating with his hands, babbling away about the all too familiar and repugnant problem concerning a piano.

Aha, the Board of Education had requisitioned his piano? Great. That's the way it should be. Understandably, he wanted the piano returned. His Olia had once wanted to enter the conservatory... Sure, sure... He was asking Kost, actually this sweet 'Konstiantyn Petrovych', to intercede on his behalf before the Board of Education... He was a communist and, though distantly related, still a relation. He begged that Kost take pity on him – this piano was his last solace. Some of their things had been confiscated, others they had to sell to survive, but the piano – his Olichka played it so beautifully... The old man's voice trembled and wheezed pathetically; if it hadn't been for the twilight, which had ensnared the room, Kost would probably have seen the tears in his eyes.

For a moment something akin to pity stirred in Horobenko's chest, but immediately it became extinguished and was replaced by an even greater indignation. He rose to his feet, placed his hand on the table and announced categorically:

"It's no use telling me all this. They were right to take the piano away from you. It couldn't have been any other way. I would have done the same, had I been in their shoes."

The old fellow flinched on the stool and hastily, as fast as his bowed feeble legs would allow him, rose to his feet.

"Konstiantyn Petrovych! I beg you! Please...! Forgive me..."

That last 'forgive me' made Kost redden. 'Forgive me'? For what? That the scum had made a fortune before? Wandering from market to market in all kinds of Nizhni Novgorods, Kazans and Kharkivs to fleece someone for an extra rouble! Perhaps 'forgive me' for the haughty aunt who had grown a double chin on that neophyte's profits? Or for his humiliated crawler of a father, who secretly dreamed of equalling his sister in wealth? 'Forgive me' for this?

Horobenko slid his hands into his trouser pockets and stood with his bare feet set apart.

"Citizen Poltavsky," he purposely avoided using the fellow's name and patronymic, saying 'citizen' slowly and with emphasis, "do you really think that I will defend the bourgeoisie, even if they happen to be relatives of my father?"

"What 'bourgeoisie'! You can see for yourself what it's like for us now…" The old fellow stopped himself short and slipped a tearful note into his voice:

"Konstiantyn Petrovych, please help us out…"

"I'm telling you firmly, this can never be. Understand? I'm a communist! Didn't you know that…?"

The old man stepped forward and stretched his hands out toward Horobenko.

"I understand, of course… You're certain… of your ideals, so to speak… But…"

The old man choked, inhaled through his nose with a loud sniffle, and quickly slipped his hand into his pocket, feeling his way there with trembling fingers along his coat seam. Horobenko shuddered and took a step back in amazement. 'He wants to give me money?! A bribe…?' he thought.

He almost shouted:

"Listen, leave my apartment please. And I'll ask you this one last time to desist with these visits. If you want to talk, there's the office…"

The old man pulled out a dirty handkerchief from his pocket and wiped his tearful eyes. Then silently, hunched over and thudding loudly with his old shoes across the floor, he left the room.

Before he reached the door, something creaked behind the door and there was a rustle. That was Paraska Fedotovna hurrying to her room after having eavesdropped on their conversation by the door with baited breath.

VIII

The Board of Education secretary bent over the director's chair much too courteously and lay the minutes on the desk. He did this very quietly and cautiously, as if fearing that the minutes might be scattered like a house of cards.

"Please, Ivan Yosypovych… The minutes to the pedagogical council meeting. You'll have to forgive me – they're still in Russian, but you know…"

The secretary's voice took on an intimate tone and dropped to a whisper: "This pedagogical technical institute of ours is really… It'll have to be taken in hand. The old elements have remained there, the specialists…" The secretary spread his arms apart and grimaced.

Ivan Radchenko began to leaf through the minutes carelessly, oblivious to the secretary's efforts. He skimmed over the lines with his screwed-up short-sighted eyes, and with each page loud remarks left his big mouth:

"…Ridiculous…! How can they discuss 'the material standing of the pedagogues' at a meeting of the pedagogical council…?! And here they go again… And what's this…? What rubbish is this?!"

Radchenko's voice made an unpleasant crackle and filled the room, as if someone was splitting dried pine logs.

Radchenko threw the last minutes to one side and picked up a pencil; then he suddenly struck his fist against the desk and, without turning around, told the secretary:

"Yeah… I nearly forgot. What is the language of instruction in the technical institute?"

The secretary shuffled from foot to foot and reverently picked up the minutes.

"You see, Ivan Yosypovych, things aren't quite normalized yet. There is no specific regulation. Even when Comrade Kudriavtsev was director here, I told him that Khanov had to be removed... He isn't the right man for the job, and besides..."

Radchenko rudely interrupted him:

"I'm asking you what language the students are being taught in?" and amazed, he looked at the secretary with his watery grey eyes. The secretary broke off in mid-sentence, but immediately regained his composure and said in a hushed voice:

"Some of the teachers lecture in Ukrainian, the rest still run classes in Russian."

Radchenko grabbed the telephone receiver and barked at the secretary:

"Get an order out: from the new academic year all pedagogues are to teach in Ukrainian before lunch, and after lunch – in Russian... That clear? That's all...! Comrade! One-fifteen... Organization instructor? Listen Semyonov, it appears you have..."

The secretary collected the minutes and asked Radchenko timidly:

"Maybe it's better to write that all classes be conducted in Ukrainian? All the teachers need to be squeezed..."

Radchenko glanced angrily at the secretary and, without replying, continued to mumble into the receiver. The secretary wilted and left the office on tip-toe.

Horobenko studied Radchenko's face. This face changed animatedly – his eyebrows, eyes, mouth, chin and even his hair and ears kept moving the whole time, making it seem as if there wasn't a telephone receiver before Radchenko, but a live person with whom he was arguing. Viewed differently, this was a dangerous madman talking with himself.

Horobenko didn't like this, and began to study Radchenko's face more closely:

'Who is he, this Radchenko?'

The question surfaced quite illogically, for Horobenko already knew a little about him from various rumours.

He was sent here from the provincial centre where, it seemed, he had connections, acquaintances and friends. Radchenko was a former Borotbist,[16] and it was obvious that after the liquidation of Borotbism all kinds of national prejudices ceased to exist for him.

He had this innate quality of always creating a commotion wherever he was. What else? His habit of rummaging through other people's papers and talking much too loudly, showed him to be an independent person, and quite insolent at that. Just why he had appeared in this district backwater – no one knew. The Party membership treated him ingratiatingly, though with caution.

People stopped being directly interested in him, he was drafted into the board of the local *Izvestii – News of the District Party Committee, Executive Committee and Trade-Union Council*, appointed director to the Board of Education, and people became accustomed to disregarding the creak and crackle of his voice. Only at Party meetings, when Radchenko had the floor, were notes passed to the presidium, demanding that regulations be adhered to. Radchenko had been in the organization only a week, but despite all his shortcomings, his negatives and positives, he was already 'one of the boys'.

---

16   Ukrainian Communist Party (Borotbist) – a national communist party, which existed under various names between 1918 and 1920.

But then really, all this was not important. There was something else. Horobenko rested his fingers on his temple, screwed up his eyes and understood.

Radchenko was to become the spotlight, which would highlight Kost's national attitudes. This was comical, strange and funny, but it was true. Before, when only Horobenko had been 'pro-Ukrainian' here, this side of him had not manifested itself, he could attack and destroy it within himself. But now, with the appearance of this Radchenko, who had the knack of immediately making everyone feel he was 'one of them' – everything would assume a different trajectory. Radchenko's membership in the organization would put Horobenko's every move under the microscope.

Kost Horobenko thought sadly: 'How good it would be if Radchenko wasn't here… If he wasn't about at all, if he didn't exist…'

Radchenko replaced the receiver with a crash and moved closer to the desk.

"Yeah… so now, Comrade Horobenko… you'll start teaching Ukrainian at the teacher's courses."

Horobenko rubbed his forehead and said wearily:

"I don't feel competent in this area, I can't be seen to be a dilettante."

"What do you mean, 'dilettante'?" Radchenko raised his bushy eyebrows in amazement. "We need to send at least one of our people there. There's not one communist at the courses."

Horobenko wanted to object one more time, but Radchenko slapped his hand on the table, as usual, not letting him speak.

"We can't send a Petliurite there, eh! Clear? That's all. Negotiate the hours with Khanov."

Radchenko was inclined to an American pace of doing things and strove for speed.

He was about to rush off somewhere, but the telephone rang and Radchenko's 'Hello!' filled the room with a sputter. The receiver crackled away, but there was no voice at the other end. Radchenko swore and threw the receiver down on the desk. Then he grabbed his briefcase and cap, and dashed off to the general office. Near the door he turned sharply and said to Horobenko:

"Yeah! We'll still have to talk about political instruction in the outlying districts... The hell knows what's going on there – nothing is happening...!" And cursing under his breath, Radchenko disappeared through the door.

Horobenko came out into the street. The midday sun flooded the street with oppressiveness and lethargy, but Horobenko moved along, satisfied that all was quiet about him at last, and Radchenko's voice had stopped creaking in his ear. And yet his weary mind still could not be free of Radchenko. He imagined Radchenko standing there on his short legs, eyes popping out, ready to swear... Who did Radchenko remind him of...? Aha: that Russian children's story about the adventures of a crocodile and the brave high-school student Vanya:

> *Through the streets there did stroll*
> *A crocodile bold.*
> *There he strolled,*
> *Speaking Turkish all day long,*
> *But to speak Turkish here*
> *Is strictly forbidden.*

Really, with his long mouth, grey goggly eyes and distinct pupils, and his disproportionate body, Radchenko did resemble a crocodile. They must have teased him in school. Actually – in the seminary. For Radchenko was the son of a priest. And he wasn't even Radchenko, but, as Slavina had learnt from somewhere – Voznesensky. Radchenko was only a pseudonym. And there was a reason. The surname was derived from the Ukrainian word *rada*, meaning council. Obviously alluding to the Workers', Peasants' and Red Army Council of Deputies.

Horobenko stopped at a street corner and checked his watch. It was approaching five. He turned left into a side street and made his way along the rotting wooden footpath.

The district supply commissar, Drobot, appeared before him unexpectedly.

"Greetings, you sonofabitch!"

Drobot slapped his spade of a hand against Horobenko's dry palm, and his open mouth reeked of hooch.

At first Horobenko didn't understand the reason for Drobot's familiarity, and even stopped dead in his tracks. Drobot's hand slapped him on the shoulder, and he asked out of the blue:

"Shuffling along, are we?"

Horobenko smiled.

"Come with me to Chernyshov's!"

Drobot grabbed Horobenko by the elbow and dragged him forward. His drunken breath tickled Horobenko's right cheek somewhat unpleasantly, but he suddenly had a desire to visit Chernyshov and even quickened his step.

Things were already buzzing at Chernyshov's. When they appeared in the doorway of the room swathed in tobacco smoke, those present began to stir. Mysha Chernyshov froze in an unnatural pose, hiding his left hand somewhere deep underneath the dirty tablecloth, and looked fearfully at the door. Assured that there was no one else apart from Horobenko and Drobot, he changed in a flash. He guffawed loudly and triumphantly brought out two half-empty bottles from under the table.

"You skunks! You lowlife! To cause such panic!"

Nestorenko kicked a rumpled strip of carpet to one side with his boot and hooked the tail of a herring with his fork.

"Yeah, it's a fact: Drobot's walk is a take-off of Krycheyev."

"So what, if it's like Krycheyev's?" Horobenko heard Druzhynin's voice and was surprised. Druzhynin was the last person he expected to be here. Druzhynin rolled a cigarette and lit up. His slightly animated voice was unusually sharp as he was drunk. Druzhynin – drunk? Druzhynin seemed to sense Horobenko's thoughts, even though he didn't look him in the eye. He said to Nestorenko:

"What's Krycheyev to me – a prior, and I'm a monk, or what? Yeah, I like to have the odd drink and they can all go to…"

"Our Party statutes don't stipulate that we can't drink hooch!" chuckled Mysha Chernyshov, but Druzhynin interrupted him:

"That's not the point. All I'm saying is, don't lie. If you drink, then say that you do! Just don't hide your bottles under the table, you swine! There's no harm in you having your drink. But respect yourself, otherwise you're…"

Mysha Chernyshov interjected mirthfully:

"Otherwise, you're a crawling rotter!"

"A hungry belly has no ears," Drobot boomed in his deep voice and poured himself half a bottle. "Brother, I've just squeezed the first five tonnes of produce allotment from Mykhailivka Rural District."

Drobot upended the glass and emptied it without blinking.

Then he wiped his whitish moustache and told another supply commissar's joke:

"You can't suck bread out of a finger, but you can pump it out of a kulak!"

Drobot placed his fat briefcase stuffed with papers on his knees and set about tearing up a herring with his fingers.

Nestorenko sidled up to Chernyshov and resumed their interrupted conversation, speaking in broken Russian:

"I still don't understand: how can Marx collide with the Earth? As long as the Earth's existed, nothing like that has happened."

Mysha Chernyshov deliberately corrected him:

"Not 'Marx', Nestorenko, but 'Mars' – it's the name of a planet. Understand?"

"Well, yeah, I realize it's a planet, but why should it fly toward Earth?"

Horobenko chuckled to himself. But immediately checked himself and became more serious:

'It's terribly bourgeois to laugh at other people's illiteracy.'

Nestorenko was still worried about Mars and continued to quiz Chernyshov:

"So what's this then – if it falls onto Earth it can destroy everything?"

Back in the times when he was an apprentice in Povzer's printing establishment, Mysha Chernyshov was drawn to all things unusual and unnatural. He was attracted to human and animal monsters with many legs, two heads, one eye or completely eyeless, Siamese twins, women with beards. Mysha Chernyshov had once been awfully interested why Halley's comet hadn't collided with the earth in the end, as had been predicted. Actually, Halley's Comet had disillusioned him. Which was why Chernyshov did not believe in Mars now, however for Nestorenko he painted the grimmest of perspectives.

"Yeah, brother, Mars isn't a pound of raisins for you. Just think, Nestorenko: that thing comes hurtling along, a thousand times bigger than Earth, and suddenly – splat! And no more Spaniards!"

Chernyshov illustrated this by slapping himself on his forehead, and added:

"Oh! There won't be a thing left after that…"

Nestorenko asked again:

"Nothing at all?"

Chernyshov replied offendedly:

"What d'you think: just try to hit something like that!"

Nestorenko rested his head on his hand and became sorrowfully contemplative. Drobot ran his eyes about the room, as if looking for something, and said capriciously:

"How come I don't see Popynaka?"

Mysha Chernyshov stirred on the sofa.

"The devil knows that Popynaka… He seems to be a fighting fellow, so to speak, and mixes with Party committee members too, but…"

"Rubbish," Drobot said authoritatively. "Popynaka should have been dragged here."

Nestorenko jangled his spurs under the table and decided to add his bit to the conversation:

"I saw Popynaka this morning with that Radchenko – they were riding along in the communal-farm buggy."

Mysha Chernyshov suddenly flinched:

"We should have invited Radchenko, comrades…"

"I don't like him, he's a smart aleck," Drobot replied sharply, smearing a slice of rye bread with thick linden honey.

Chernyshov came out in enthusiastic defence:

"Nonsense! Nothing of the sort... He's a good lad. You only have to know how to approach him. But here's what's interesting..." Chernyshov's attraction to all things unnatural was awoken once more, and he enthusiastically, even a little secretively, grabbed hold of his objective.

"He's all right, only he has an unlucky hand for wenches. Just think – he's ruined three already..."

Nestorenko was intrigued by this and moved his chair closer to Chernyshov. Drawing his small head with its black shock of hair and small green eyes from his collar, he asked:

"What d'you mean?"

Chernyshov eagerly explained:

"He's built something weird. While his woman is still pregnant – everything is all right, but the moment she goes into labour, that's it... His third woman died in hospital in Kharkiv this spring. They pulled the dead child out with forceps."

Nestorenko jangled his spurs once more and said in amazement:

"So that's how it is...!"

Drobot was eating, relishing the honey. He chewed assiduously with his strong jaws and licked the edges from which large drops of honey slowly dripped. However, several drops had slipped out from under his tongue, falling onto his knees and silently plopped onto his briefcase. A minute later this was repeated a second time. Horobenko noticed the shiny viscous spots on the dull leather of the briefcase and recalled those first five tonnes of produce allotment from Mykhailivka Rural District. He suddenly thought:

'I wonder if they also take an allotment of honey from the bee-keepers...'

Mysha Chernyshov reminded Drobot of his assessment of Radchenko and finished animatedly:

"No! He's an ace lad. A golden lad. Except perhaps that he speaks the 'language' at times." Smiling, Chernyshov looked at Horobenko and, as if on cue, everyone else turned their heads in the same direction.

Horobenko became confused and could not think of anything to say right away.

Drobot wiped his sticky hands on the tablecloth and, adding a little intimacy to his deep voice, moved awkwardly up to Horobenko.

"Tell me, Horobenko, is it true that in nineteen eighteen you executed sailors in Kyiv?"

Horobenko forced a smile, but said firmly:

"No."

However, catching Nestorenko's stern, sidelong glance, he was unable to allay his inner anxiety and turned to Drobot:

"I simply don't understand what kind of question this is?"

Drobot slid his hands deep into his pockets and placed his feet wide apart. A cunning smile played on his greasy lips.

"Own up – did it happen?"

Horobenko looked up uncomfortably at Drobot:

"What nonsense is this? Why this sudden…"

Drobot grew angry:

"Because you're one sonofabitch…!"

Horobenko blushed deeply and rose to his feet.

"And what does that mean, comrade?"

Mysha Chernyshov seriously began to fear a fight might break out and, jumping to his feet, rushed up to them.

"What are you up to here? I don't understand! That's enough! Sit down, you crawling rotter," he jostled Drobot jokingly, and the fellow settled back onto his chair.

Mysha Chernyshov turned around to face Horobenko:

"Drive the rotters off…! Well, so you were for 'independence' one time, but so what!"

Morose and silent, Druzhynin piped up unexpectedly from his corner. Since he hadn't spoken a word for a long time, everyone now turned to face him:

"What's there to figure out – was he or wasn't he! Well, even if he was, what's better then: the fact that he's our comrade now or that he remains a staunch chauvinist separatist? There are no people who are completely black or white, brother! If you look closely – most people are grey…"

No one said anything in answer to Druzhynin's words, however the strained atmosphere in the room was immediately defused.

Horobenko felt like giving Druzhynin's hand a hearty shake.

IX

His lecture as part of the teachers' course was due to begin at ten and now it was only nine. Actually, it was nine according to the clock, but in fact, according to the sun, it was six.

Each month the clock hands were moved, and the clock slowly lost its power as a former administrative standard. People reverted to the distant past and orientated themselves by the sun. By its beautiful, joyous rising, and sad, but no less beautiful setting.

With yellowed faces and souls, dried up like old archival paper, former civil servants who were now Soviet employees, saw the sun in all its grandiose beauty for the first time.

They were short of bread, millet and oil, had worn away their last shreds of clothing, their rumbling stomachs drowned out their thoughts; they slowly lost everything, including all hope of any change for the better, but they were never short of sun. There was enough sun everywhere. It seemed as if the new authorities had somehow increased the length of the day, cutting the night back to a bare minimum.

Kost Horobenko was overjoyed at this too. He walked along the sunny side of the street on purpose and bathed his uncovered head in the sunshine like a child. The sun caressed his forehead and his hair, gently running its invisible soft fingers over his neck and under his open collar, its rays melting away doubts, suffering and grief.

Then his mind and body fused into a single harmonious whole, and the familiar detestable houses in this district town, the local people and the whole boundless world seemed a better place. Horobenko's soul too became devoid of malice, and envy, and suspicion: a single beautiful sunny word – love – subconsciously and imperceptibly welled in his chest and filled every corner of it.

He would never utter it now, but he had felt its touch. He had felt its eternal beauty and immortality, and this brought him joy. There were eternal beautiful things, before which countless people had bowed on the long path of history, and they would continue to bow before them as long as people were people and the Earth remained the Earth.

There was mass poverty, misery, destruction, famine was drawing closer… He had his own hidden pains, disagreements and failures…

This was now, today. But years would pass, ages, millennia – and these would all disappear… this was understandable – the ruins would become covered with new buildings, humanity would suffer poverty and hunger many a time, and against the background of this small and trifling personal pains and insults would become lost… The time would come, and there would be no Ukraine, perhaps there would be no nations at all, but there would still be the sun, and love.

This sun! This eternally youthful, forever joyous morning sun! Why, when it shone like it did now, when it caressed his unlocked soul and his unbuttoned chest, did he recall Nadia so instantly, so unexpectedly…?!

For some reason the sun's rays decided to rest on the bulging muscle on his neck. Warming it most of all. Even seeming to massage it.

He remembered: Nadia used to love that muscle. Her hand, that loving hand which would no longer rise from the grave, paused at this muscle many a time when it stroked his neck. And then her large dark eyes, penetrated by the transparent shadow of gentle sorrow common to all southern people, rested on his profile. And quietly, silently, they watched him very, very closely. As if wanting to guess something and, without having guessed a thing, they had gone to the grave… Nadia had died.

And once more Horobenko thought that this was very good. Not even because she would have been alien to all this, not being a member of the Party. No. That was a secondary consideration.

Here was what was most important: the millstones of time would have ground up the fresh grain of feelings which had once welled up in both of them and their conjugal life would not have been an intoxicating wine, only powdery flour, sticky dough and, who knows, perhaps even chaff… Now Nadia would always remain the way she was in those distant, irretrievable days. Nadia had died, but she would continue to live as a beautiful memory of his first love, a pure memory of the first woman he had known.

This memory would live inside him. It had to live, for it was the only thing he still had from his past.

And this was no vow of male virginity, this was no sentimental 'till death us do part', this was something very human and quite real, but it was after all something bigger than them. Because one certainly could not forget one's first woman, one who had been a virgin before meeting you, and Nadia, Nadia…

Horobenko thought timidly:

'What would I have done with her now, when love seems to have been abolished and the bed has replaced the best relationships between the sexes…'

And just as a clumsy whitish cloud appeared out of nowhere and covered the sun, Horobenko suddenly saw the reality of yesterday, the day before, and the previous week, and the reality of people as they were.

He asked himself:

'What's all this leading to?'

The sun melted away the small cloud and it continued on its endless heavenly trek as a scattered light mist, while the sun's warm rays played on Kost's neck with renewed vitality.

Then, without further thought, a long-since ready, but forgotten reply surfaced:

'These people, these official friends of yours – they're better than you thought.'

The Party was no arsenal of saints. But therein lay its strength, its unique messianism, that from the most ordinary of people, those with inherent good and evil in them, it was creating a new, quite distinct tribe. A Bolshevik race...

Who would reveal the true Druzhynin to the general public? This simple, yet at the same time amiable Druzhynin? How simply, how ably he had swept aside that damned gloom of suspicion and distrust, which had secretly swirled about Kost.

And was Druzhynin alone? No. He was the symbol of those other potential Druzhynins, who were still making their way, but would inevitably arrive one day.

And then there was Mysha Chernyshov. He was obviously a shallow person, a drunk, and all earthly sins undoubtedly pursued him, but...

This was incomprehensible too. Chernyshov knew not only about the Prosvita and the National Alliance branch. There was more. This same Chernyshov, having once worked as an apprentice in Povzer's printing establishment, would have typeset business cards for Horobenko's father. And once even... it was in about grade six in high school, Kost had foolishly ordered business cards for himself.

Horobenko felt painfully annoyed at this recollection. He even wanted to let out a groan, to somehow erase those naive business cards in high school from his memory, which now pained his heart.

Theoretically Chernyshov should be harbouring, at least in his memory, a hostility toward him, a class hatred. For in fact back then the fellow had been a proletarian and Kost, though not consciously, was an exploiter of the people.

But there was none of this. Chernyshov was his comrade now. He even showed a certain amount of affection for Kost. What kind of 'general pardon' was this?

That magical word 'Party' floated before Horobenko once more. And probably for the first time he felt consciously and concretely a member of its enormous and unusual collective...

Horobenko had arrived early for the courses. Young female teachers were already walking the passages in pairs, in threes and alone, the shabby figures of old, once sedate pedagogues skulked along cautiously and silently, but they created no noise in the building. These teachers, who for long years (some obstinately, others with nervous exhaustion) had fought in class with natural childish laughter, shouts and clamour, didn't know how to be noisy themselves, they only rustled along quietly. And Horobenko felt strange walking along the passage past this quiet, seemingly constrained crowd.

This passage had known other times. This building had housed the Pedagogical Technical School, it was the former home of his high school.

By some unknown tradition the lecturers at the teachers' courses now congregated in the 'staff room' before the start of lessons. These were mostly the old high-school teachers. Here sat Borysenko, the slightly frayed former lion of the town's damsels, the handsome geography teacher from whom Kost had received a 'fail' on several occasions. The history teacher, Makaron,[17] who would ask the high-school students: 'How long did the Thirty Year War last?', and then there was Gander – the Ukrainian-language teacher Prykhodko. All of them had remained in the 'staff room', like shabby museum relics of some forgotten era.

Khanov, the head of the courses, courteously stepped forward toward Horobenko, rubbing his fists together before shaking hands, and informed him:

"Your lesson is in ten minutes, Konstiantyn Petrovych, but in the meantime we've a small family conference, so to speak."

Khanov was the former director of another high school. Horobenko did not know him. Khanov acted prudently toward Horobenko, for he was a communist, a goat in a sheepfold, so to speak. But he had to accommodate him somehow. In fact, he had to win him over to their side. This could even be useful: why, for instance, didn't teachers receive white flour, while the Supply Committee employees had received thirty kilograms each!

Khanov tugged at his greenish, musty beard and adjusted his gold-rimmed glasses.

"…Here, see, as part of our ration we've received three yards of cloth… What do we do with it – you can't divide it among everyone…?"

"Raffle it off," Gander growled angrily from his corner.

---

17   The nickname literally means "Macaroni".

The long-legged historian, Makaron, slipped his dry knotty hand under his vest, sullied with borshch and wax, and asked sceptically:

"What kind of cloth is it – some rubbish obviously, eh?"

Kost's teachers did not hide their feelings from him. Out of old habit they sensed their superiority over the young lecturer of Ukrainian, over this former student of theirs.

Borysenko sprawled out in his armchair and continued telling Makaron in Russian:

"Just you imagine, Nikanor Ivanovich, the Board of Education secretary hands me a form: 'Fill it out.' Magnificent! I read there: which party do you belong to? I reply: excuse me, I'll leave that question out... I don't understand them. What does it matter which party I belong to? Such stupid questions! Yeah, I consider myself above any party!"

Khanov threw a fearful sidelong glance over his glasses at Horobenko. Borysenko caught this look and gave Khanov a carefree smile with his kind grey eyes. Disturbed, Khanov shuffled through his papers, while Borysenko continued to voice his indignation in Russian:

"Amazing prejudices…!"

'Boors! Educated boors!' Horobenko fumed inside but remained silent and only reddened slightly.

Another lecturer responded from behind a cupboard:

"They say the Poles have already taken Kyiv…"

Taking no notice at all of Horobenko, as if he wasn't even present, Makaron mumbled spitefully:

"*Comrade* Budenny[18] is hurrying to the rescue. He'll show them!"

---

18   Russian cavalry commander.

Borysenko tried to make a joke of it:

"Somehow our Budenny is already too humdrum.[19]"

The pun turned out quite awkward and only Borysenko laughed, the rest merely smiled.

But this was enough for Horobenko. This arrogant ignorance of his presence, their indifference that a communist was sitting among them – this irritated him to no end. Oh, these beadles were aware of the importance of his subject! Lectures in Ukrainian language in the teachers' courses were just as much a joke to them as those three yards of material assigned to be shared among seven people, or the new educational measures of the authorities, or the authorities themselves, and this whole period in general…

Why were they so certain that he would cover for their hissing, remaining silent in the Party? Why? 'I'll go and tell them everything!'

Out of civility, or perhaps pity, they at least didn't poke fun at him yet, a self-made teacher… That would have been all he needed, the devil take them!

Kost itched to yell at them, to curse them in the most obscene language.

He looked defiantly into Makaron's cold eyes and noticed that the fellow was still wearing the same jacket he used to wear when he taught at the high school.

Something bridled Horobenko's anger and irritation. He came up to Khanov and said coldly:

"I won't be giving my lecture today. I've remembered that there are pressing Party matters to attend to."

"Please, please," Khanov rose ingratiatingly and hastened to shake Horobenko's hand in farewell.

---

19   A play on the Russian word *budnichnyi*, meaning humdrum.

"Please, please, Konstiantyn Petrovych… And when shall I reschedule it for?"

"I'll let you know."

The pedagogues became quiet and looked incomprehensibly at Horobenko. The 'Party matters' tickled their ears disagreeably and even saddened them. It suddenly became far too quiet in the 'staff room', and Horobenko's hurried steps sounded hostile and much too alien.

Only Makaron asked Khanov to let him see the cloth they had received.

X

Kost caught Radchenko as he was dashing out of Socialist Education and heading over to inspect the old theatre building, in order to reorganize the arts in town.

Radchenko didn't want to stop, greeting Horobenko on the run with his eyes and a slight wave of the hand, but Horobenko said officially and even curtly:

"Just hold on there a moment, comrade. I've just come from the courses. The place is a hotbed of concealed counter-revolution. Especially this Borysenko… They badly need a political commissar there."

"Ah, the scum! What did they say?"

In fits and starts Horobenko painted a picture of Borysenko. As usual, Radchenko stared at him with watery eyes and swore abhorrently several times.

"Great. I'll tame that scum…!" he retorted finally and raced off down the street, waving his free hand about.

Horobenko watched him go for a minute or so, then looked indifferently at the high bell tower which appeared inopportunely before him, and suddenly felt an emptiness inside.

The relief he felt after speaking to Radchenko took away with it the rest of his thoughts. These thoughts became entangled and hung limply like rags. There remained a sediment of dissatisfaction and disappointment.

Horobenko wandered off down the street. He wanted to amuse himself a little. However, the detritus would not leave his soul. On the contrary. Out of that filth something suddenly slipped out and took on a defined form.

'A denunciation?'

He felt bad and even ashamed.

"To stoop so low… To go to Radchenko and tell on them… You could have stood up there in the 'staff room' and told them all off openly, even simply forbidden them to carry on like that… It would have created a scandal, you would have felt very uncomfortable, but at least it would have been honest… 'Honest'?"

Horobenko paused and smiled to himself:

"What twaddle! Who can tell now what is honest and what is vile?"

'In Borysenko's opinion one's very membership of the Party is dishonest, but in my opinion it's vile to be dependent on the authorities for one's ration, and then to ridicule them furtively…! There can be no common path with these people. They are the rubbish which lies underfoot and are an obstacle to progress.'

A voice seemed to whisper in Horobenko's ear:

'They must be destroyed…'

Horobenko returned to the Board of Education, grabbed a warrant, and went off to his high school physics teacher to requisition a microscope for the workers' evening classes.

The physics teacher lived nearby in his own small bungalow, hidden behind bushes of lilac. Horobenko hurried across the yard and entered the house.

The old, bald physics teacher appeared before Horobenko in a torn Tussar silk shirt, his middle girded with a piece of rope.

He wanted to ask him to sit down and hurried to grab a chair, but Horobenko stunned the physics teacher with his dry official tone:

"I've come to requisition your microscope," and he showed the physics teacher the warrant. The physics teacher's gentle face, with its nice apple complexion, stretched and froze. He seemed to turn to stone. Something forced Horobenko to look at the physics teacher one more time. His kind half-closed eyes and face crisscrossed with wrinkles, coloured by an ashen beard, were alluring. One could look into his face and feel one's gaze and mind relax.

Horobenko relented and looked. The physics teacher's face was filled with pain, insult and amazement. He couldn't look the physics teacher in the eye. Horobenko bit his lip and turned away.

If only the physics teacher had sworn, shouted, stamped his feet, and argued with him – that would have made it much easier.

But the gentle physics teacher hadn't been like that at the high school and nor did he act this way now.

The physics teacher left the room, taking large shaky steps and a minute later returned with the microscope.

He looked at the clean shining microscope tubes, sighed and handed it silently to Horobenko. Horobenko wanted to hand over the warrant, but the physics teacher had already disappeared behind a curtain.

Horobenko looked about the room and lay the warrant on the nearest chair. Then hastily, as if fearing that the physics teacher might come running after him, he rushed outside with the microscope.

Faded and old, like the physics teacher himself, Kashtan, whom Horobenko had known from his high school days, crawled out from his kennel to warm himself in the sun. He noticed Horobenko and, wagging his tail, ran to the porch. Poor old dog! He didn't even have an inkling what harm had just been inflicted on his master.

Scratching the ground with his hind paw, Kashtan began to fawn upon Horobenko as best he knew, licking his hand and rubbing his muzzle against his pants.

Horobenko paused involuntarily to pat the dog. He wanted to grab its shaggy head near the ears and shake it about as he had done before, but the microscope in his left hand prevented him from doing so. Horobenko felt embarrassed and pained. He became embarrassed in front of the dog, which sincerely granted him its canine caresses, not sensing any hostility in him. These caresses were stolen – and Horobenko immediately made off for the gate.

He felt sorry for the naive dog and the poor physics teacher, and himself.

"These are all palliatives! Miserable palliatives…! You're not whipping the horses, but only the rotten, good-for-nothing thills."

A voice laughed inside Horobenko, mocking him:

"You've taken away an old fellow's last pride and joy to prove that you're a Bolshevik? Ha-ha-ha…! Who will you prove this to? Perhaps yourself? Rubbish! You know full well that this isn't the point. What is some microscope to the revolution! You puny, egotistical soul! You want to buy yourself a new conscience by inflicting misery on people? That's cheap! Far too cheap… This is bought only with – remember that sleepless night? – only with blood! With death!"

Horobenko hurried along the edge of the sidewalk and his hand holding the microscope was stretched unnaturally forward. The microscope stuck out before him like a damnation and burned his palm. But there was nowhere to hide it. Horobenko tried to evade the occasional passer-by, but this didn't work. People still passed him, and their gazes rested on the microscope.

Horobenko did not turn around, but it seemed to him that everyone stopped behind him and whispered:

"He's carried off the microscope! The microscope… There he goes!"

Horobenko quickened his step.

"These are all useless palliatives. Those requisitioned pianos, and cupboards, and books, and this microscope! Something else is needed. I need to go to the Party Committee and – that's enough! Send me to join the Cheka, I can't go on like this…! They took into consideration my 'intellectualism' when they appointed me to the Cultural Section of the trade union. I need to speak frankly with Krycheyev… Only would I be able to work for the Cheka?"

And Horobenko immediately replied:

"To work in the Cheka, one has to execute people all the same. One first needs a few drops of blood on the earth, otherwise there will be hypocrisy, otherwise everything will be lies…"

Horobenko stepped onto the puny wooden bridge across the narrow, foul river, which flowed through the town. Some fellow walked across the bridge and disappeared in the willows. Horobenko suddenly stopped. He caught his breath and suddenly looked about. It was deserted. Down below, breaking through the duckweed, the dirty water glistened in the sunshine. Horobenko looked about stealthily once more and tossed the microscope with all his might into the river, as if it had been stolen.

Somewhere far away there was a splash and again everything became quiet. Horobenko ran from the bridge and made his way to the trade-union Cultural Section.

XI

With his whip handle the old peasant adjusted the shaft chain, which had shifted on the thill, rolled himself an enormously thick cigarette in some newsprint, and merrily lightly whipped his nag.

"Giddy-up, there...!"

The nag flicked its burr-encrusted tail to one side and trotted off for a few steps, then again continued in its way lazily up the hill.

Slavina became silent for only a minute; she fussed about, spreading out the truss of hay under her and drew in her thin, skinny legs right up to her chest, which made the knees under her skirt appear even sharper, and it seemed as if they were capable of painfully pricking someone. Horobenko transferred his gaze to Druzhynin's muddy boots with holes, which hung down from the ladderbeam, and to interrupt Slavina's incessant chatter he asked the old peasant:

"Is that Fedorivka over there already?"

"*Da*, a little ways along this sand and we'll pass the boulder, and there'll be the Fedorivka windmills."

However, Slavina was not even thinking of abandoning her subject. On the contrary, she considered it her duty to continue persuading the old peasant to become an atheist. She was being shaken unmercifully on the cart, being unaccustomed to such travel, she squirmed and grimaced at every pothole. She had long since felt as if her insides had become terribly entangled, however the presence of the two party members galvanized her. Slavina wanted to prove to them that she wasn't at all made of "white dough" and this harvest wagon, and this road they had taken along the damned endless byways just to avoid the bandits lurking in the woods along the direct route – all this was nothing to her. And so Slavina took a hold of herself and without any small-talk or reason, had been expounding her anti-religious diatribe to the old peasant.

The fellow turned out to be bright and good-natured. He completely surprised Horobenko by readily joining in the conversation, however he hardly argued with Slavina, avoiding decisive replies. He insinuated more and joked, than argued.

"Well, of course. As the saying goes: so long as there are people, there will always be a priest. But then, when one thinks about it…"

Slavina interrupted him in Russian:

"Hold on, comrade. Firstly, let's focus on the question of religion. For example, Karl Marx said: religion is the opium of the people."

The old peasant had either misunderstood her last words or simply had not heard them properly, for he suddenly had an urge to agree with Slavina and, tugging at the reins, he said briskly:

"Yes, it's true, everything now is for the people."

Druzhynin burst into loud guffaws, while Horobenko smiled and looked more affably at Slavina. Slavina became embarrassed and blushed. She felt insulted and awkward because of the muzhik's failure to understand her and itched to stem her own confusion. She squirmed and, disconcerted, tried to explain to the old peasant:

"Religion is, you see, comrade, above all… well, how can I explain it to you…? It's an illusion… You're a man who…"

The old peasant interpreted Druzhynin's laughter in his own way. He sighed deeply and turned to Slavina:

"Well, I can't say whether it's a 'lusion' or not, but even I, by God, wouldn't be attending church if it was certain…" The fellow flashed gentle grey eyes from under his knitted brows and moved closer to Slavina:

"All that you've been saying is of course right… Well, good and fine if there's nothing up there (the old peasant shook a rein, pointing into the sky)! But what if there is…?" The old peasant moved up to Slavina and looked intently into her face:

"Well, what if, when you die, it's all really up there?!"

Slavina had no ready answer and the old peasant spread his arms apart helplessly and once more moved forward to the nosebag packed with oats.

"Come on, you nag! Dragging your feet there! Giddy-up…"

The old peasant cracked the whip in the air and uttered firmly, though in a lowered voice:

"No, no matter what, it's mother better to go to church. Gives you more peace of mind after all…"

The old peasant's summation again lit up a smile on Horobenko's face. However, the smile was diluted with irony, and then he was seized with acute impatience – when would this nonsensical conversation finally end! He was irritated by Slavina's language too, which the old peasant could not understand, and her inept use of words, her inability to approach the old peasant simply, ordinarily. He even rejoiced that all this had ended as an anecdote, but at the same time he was afraid Slavina would once more try to convince the old peasant. At times he felt sorry for Slavina. This unneeded woman, quite ugly in appearance, with sharp bony knees, was setting herself up for ridicule. She kept mumbling awkward words, and the old peasant laughed at her in his heart. Oh, this was a cunning old peasant! Kost could picture him well. For him Slavina's anaemic words were like peas being thrown against a wall. Intellectually, even on his peasant scale, he was a whole head higher than Slavina.

Kost imagined perfectly how the old peasant would tell everyone in the village about this shorn, foolish 'communist' woman and make fun of her. Bah, he would make fun of them all. They were her comrades. Once again, he felt sorry for Slavina and was indignant at the sight of the peasant's patched cloak: you'll cry your eyes out yet!

Horobenko looked at the sumptuous field of wheat and, as usual, it soothed him. The untiring mischievous wind drove wave after wave across it. The waves rushed after each other, until they broke off at the fresh stubble, however the wind was oblivious to that: it raced back along the ridges dividing the fields and generated more waves. The harvest was beginning, and the first shocks were already throwing a light shadow on summer. These shocks and the stubble always made one feel sad. A growing pity filled one's chest and one felt inexplicably sorry about something. The summer, the heat, or one's own passing days? Who knows? These shocks would give birth to an incomprehensible longing, and later, when the autumn rain pattered on the roof in the evening, this longing would beckon unhappy autumnal conclusions with a senile hand...

Horobenko bit through a dry grass stalk and mused.

Reapers were having lunch by the roadside. Having reached them, the old peasant turned off to the left to bypass their empty cart and unharnessed emaciated nags. As they emerged on the far side, pulling out of a deep rut, they dallied a little. The reapers watched them questioningly. When the cart drew up to them, the fellow on the end winked to the old peasant carter:

"Doing business there, Danylo?"

However, the carter refrained from any jokes. He stopped his nag for some reason and greeted them:

"Good-day, may the Lord help you…"

Some devil prompted Slavina to join in the conversation again:

"Good-day, comrades!" She looked at the fresh sheaves of mown wheat and said condescendingly in Russian:

"You've got a fine crop of rye this year."

The reapers burst into guffaws and the carter, as if embarrassed for his passengers, grumbled:

"Come on, this is wheat!"

Slavina whispered guiltily to herself:

"Can it really be…? How could I have been mistaken…?"

"Of course, you're 'mistaken', you've probably never even sown it!" someone said from the back, smiling malevolently.

Horobenko had long been embarrassed about Slavina, and the reapers' jocular laughter unnerved him. He tapped the carter on the shoulder:

"Hurry on. We have to get there before sunset."

The old fellow tugged at the reins and the cart continued on its way, pursued by the reapers' derisive stares.

After they had moved away, Druzhynin looked back toward the sheaves and, after a moment's thought, said to Slavina:

"*Da*, it really was wheat, not rye. That was rather unfortunate of you, Comrade Slavina. You need to tread more lightly…"

Slavina did not answer and made herself more comfortable on her seat. She was overcome with disappointment and despair.

'You can't go far in the village with these Slavinas,' Horobenko thought and angrily spat the stalk from his mouth.

It was growing dark when they reached the village.

Ahead of them a herd of cattle was kicking up the evening dust on the road as it made its way home. The cows moved phlegmatically to their respective yards, stopping outside gates and lowing monotonously. Some turned around lazily and stared stupidly at the road.

Their gazes reflected utter boredom and eternal surprise.

"I don't understand a damned thing – what's all this about?"

However, the cows did not even attempt to comprehend what it was about. They merely satisfied themselves with having witnessed the arrival of three new people in the village, and turned away from the spectacle, to begin their philosophical lowing once more.

Their lowing filled Horobenko with warmth and a special inner peace. It was gratifying to watch the cows disperse, to see the young herdsmen in muddy pants, bags over their shoulders, hurrying up the rest of the herd with switches.

The mounds of white houses and the green wool of the black poplars, sycamores and willows created an air of peace and tranquillity.

It made one want to stare blankly ahead and watch one's whole inner being fill with calmness and peace.

Horobenko even cheered up. Shevchenko's words were so true: 'A village – and the heart can rest'... Only it wasn't that village which now spread before him; a test, rather than relaxation, was awaiting Kost Horobenko. One of the countless tests on the path to becoming a 'Bolshevik', a test of life.

Horobenko lowered his numb legs onto the ladderbeam and curiously eyed the sloping strip of village houses, grey in the evening twilight.

Somewhere deep down in those stove niches, behind the cattle sheds, on the meadows, the village soul lay hidden, together with people's rusty sawn-off rifles. It was wary, suspicious and cruel. On the outside there stood gentle taciturn houses with smoke curling from some of the chimneys. These houses had probably stood unchanged since tsarist times, perhaps even since serfdom and the Cossack era... Who could tell?

Horobenko said to himself:

"I still don't know you at all, village. You are still a riddle, like my whole whimsical nation. You are foreign to me – foreign, distant and incomprehensible. In this respect I'm not far removed from Slavina..."

It was probably because he thinks every Ukrainian is a peasant deep down that Krycheyev sent me here as head of the re-election troika. Not Druzhynin, but me. That is understandable. And yet,' Horobenko smiled to himself, 'I am not a peasant after all, and there is nothing of the village in me. True, this is a little unusual for a Ukrainian, however, be warned, village – I'm not even inclined to try to understand you. I am not bowing before your lyricized houses, neat orchards, very ordinary 'darling moon' and your other inevitable accessories. I'm quite indifferent to all this now, but at times... at times I damn well feel like smashing all this to pieces... But I will rein you in you all the same, village!

Sensing the journey's end, the nag suddenly surged forward and set off at a trot. The cart clattered loudly over the hard earth and awakened the street. Children dashed out of yards and timidly hugged old posts as they curiously watched the cart. From windows beyond fences old women peered fearfully, and only rarely did a bearded male face watch them sullenly from beside a gate. These sullen looks from under scowling brows were very noticeable and became imprinted in one's memory.

The bearded faces did not augur anything good. Their eyes saw only enemies on every cart which arrived from the city. They arrived here, to these tranquil houses, with their produce allotments, levies, arrests and executions. The village had damned them and burrowed into its holes.

Horobenko suddenly thought:

"Oh, there's probably a fierce death lurking behind those looks…!"

Horobenko wholeheartedly took in those gazes, wanting to retain them for as long as possible, imprinting them on himself.

The street came to a sudden end and the cart shook its way into a square. On the left appeared the large awkward brick building of the former rural district office – now the Fedorivka Rural District Executive Committee office. The cart turned sharply toward the

old steps and columns blackened by time.

"This will be the Executive Committee then, whoa…" the carter announced without turning around, and pulled the reins toward himself.

Druzhynin jumped down from the cart and began to massage his legs. Slavina painstakingly dusted herself and mumbled something in displeasure.

"So, you'd be the re-election troika, comrades?"

Harasymenko, the Collective Farm Executive Committee chairman, quietly approached the cart in his velour cap, a pistol sitting on his belt, and placed his strong chapped hand on the ladderbeam.

Slavina carefully lowered her feet over the side and jumped, holding her breath. If Druzhynin had not caught her by the arm she would probably have fallen under the wheel, however it all ended fortuitously and, retrieving her briefcase from the hay, Slavina told Harasymenko angrily:

"Well really, your roads, comrade! They're a nightmare…"

Harasymenko slapped the ladderbeam in a businesslike fashion, however he could find no answer to justify the state of the roads and remained silent. After everyone had removed their belongings from the cart, he rested his hand on his waist and asked:

"Will you step inside the Executive Committee offices? People are assembling for a meeting right now."

Horobenko liked Harasymenko's soft, gentle speech and his level-headed manner. It contained an inner stability and confidence, as well as the reliable adroitness of an assiduous superior.

Ascending the steps alongside Harasymenko, Horobenko suddenly thought:

'How the revolution has changed people, after all! This fellow is no longer a former officer or clerk. One can rely on this man…'

Harasymenko let everyone pass into the dark passage, then unnoticeably moved ahead of them and staidly entered the 'chairman's room'.

The deep twilight had warped a black woollen fabric throughout the room. Rough words and whispers rose to the high ceiling from its dark downcast corners.

"We need a light here," Harasymenko said in the direction of the window. Everyone became silent and pricked up their ears. The Executive Committee secretary promptly fetched a miserable lamp from a cupboard and diligently set about lighting it. The lamp resisted his efforts for a long time, flickering and dying away, but at last it was lit and burned with a melancholy bluish flame.

As if emerging from a chasm, the room slowly filled with staid beards, faces and peasant cloaks.

Druzhynin sat down on a small stool and wearily leaned back against a table.

Slavina had settled down on a bench against the wall, however the elderly villagers hastily moved away, sweeping the bench with the flaps of their cloaks, as if the woman's thin figure required room for three. Slavina became confused and hastened to join Druzhynin. Making herself comfortable beside him, she heaved a sigh of relief and settled down.

The room filled with an awkward silence once more, which no one dared disturb.

Horobenko paced across the room. Elderly peasants sat against the wall, eyeing the new arrivals with sharp questioning looks. These looks tickled Horobenko unpleasantly on the temple and right hand, but he did not turn to face them. He moved to the opposite side and purposely stood with his back to them. Marx hung sedately on the wall, studying the peasant cloaks, and under him someone had stuck up the old *V.I. Lenin's Letter to the Ukrainian Peasants* with glutinous bread. These external signs of a new era among the morose old men against the walls did not yet give the place a Soviet air: outside in the darkness, two miles away, was the Vorskla River and beyond it the ancient Poltava forests, woodsmen, rebellion and death. Who could guarantee what would happen here in one, two or three hours? Horobenko turned to face the light and ran his eyes over the peasants. Although they maintained the same pose, their faces now seemed to be saying 'it's not my concern', 'we're not locals'.

'This is probably the best one could expect from them in times of trouble,' Horobenko thought. 'Although perhaps they might…'

The old peasants remained sitting in silence and all one could hear was their heavy wheezing breath. The silence was becoming unbearable for Horobenko, but he did not know how to approach these people, how to unlock their closed souls, to make them talk, speak openly and frankly to him, as if he was one of them. He felt unsettled and the figures of the elderly peasants irritated him. He strode up to Harasymenko and asked loudly:

"How's the prod-allotment going here?!"

The men in cloaks standing against the wall craned their heads greedily forward and froze.

"What do you mean?" Harasymenko did not understand straight away. "You mean the produce allotment?

"Yes, yes, the produce allotment," Horobenko said impatiently and reddened under Druzhynin's gaze.

"It's proceeding slowly, counter-revolution is still seething here… There are saboteurs – you could say they continually hinder us… There are lots of kulaks left. We have a problem with them. It's like living in the middle of a road – they stop us from organizing a good communist cell. Three new guys signed up here, but whenever there's a general meeting they don't turn up out of fear. What we need to do with the kulaks here is…" Harasymenko struck his hand heavily against his chest and firmly clenched his fist. The men against the wall looked attentively at the fist without blinking an eyelid. Harasymenko lowered his hand onto the table.

"You can't deal with them peacefully, they refuse to accept any notion of authority," he said in his usual broken Russian.

Harasymenko struggled hard to choose the right words, but kept running out of them, and so he spoke with pauses, droplets of sweat appearing on his forehead under the cracked peak of his velour cap. Horobenko liked the way he spoke. He looked at his stocky, sturdy shoulders and they seemed to him like a bridge between them and the peasant cloaks against the wall. There was still only a handful of these Harasymenkos, but how strong they were! What would the Soviet regime have done in the countryside were it not for them? The rural areas would have become a continuous impenetrable jungle. While there was even one Harasymenko in the village, there was no need to worry: he would not betray the cause, he would not look the other way, he would not leave the village. New incomprehensible words had agitated his brain, set fire to his soul, and he would continue with them in his heavy boots, without straying from his village path. 'How important these Harasymenkos are to us…!' Horobenko thought. Looking at Harasymenko and listening to his unwieldy speech made one feel more at ease, calmer. Horobenko pulled a tobacco pouch from his pocket and offered it to Harasymenko:

"Let's smoke some city tobacco."

Harasymenko wriggled his fingers and, as if excusing himself, said softly:

"I don't smoke… I've no need…" Then he raised his bearded head over the table toward the dark corner and, in the tone of a superior, said to the Executive Committee secretary:

"I want the election roll ready tomorrow."

Slavina buttoned up her small rumpled jacket and leaned over to Druzhynin:

"It would be nice to dine in some kulak home tonight…"

XII

The sun struck the small window but was unable to completely penetrate the house. It had marked out its place on the earthen floor with a golden shaft of light, however in the oven niche, on the dirty plank bed covered in black rubbish and in the corner from which several gilded gods looked sternly – there remained a stubborn twilight. Horobenko rubbed his eyes and sat up. Druzhynin and Slavina were still asleep on either side of him. Druzhynin lay spreadeagled on the hay, crumpled sacking beneath him, while his right leg (his big toe pierced by a ray of light), had made its way to the earthen floor. On the very edge of the sacking Slavina lay rolled up into a small aged fist, breathing imperceptibly. Horobenko glanced at the small lump of her body and felt sorry for her again.

"During a disaster at sea women and children are given first place on the lifeboats. So why the hell does Krycheyev plug the hole in our ark with such miserable, forlorn women…? At best, this is ridiculous, perhaps even downright cruel…"

The owners were not in the house and only a small tousled blonde head and a pair of black eyes below two small pigtails peered curiously at them from the oven. Seeing that Horobenko had woken up, the children stopped breathing completely, afraid to move.

The room was heavy with the smell of sweat, baked bread and something unfamiliar, the stench of which hung in the air and pressed down on the lungs.

Horobenko dressed hurriedly and stepped outside.

All around him everyday village life was proceeding in its usual languid, unhurried way, without gusto or feverishness.

Horobenko startled a chicken and made his way to the gate.

With a heavy step, Harasymenko was making his way across the street toward him, in the company of a blond, full-faced man in a soiled, well-worn jacket.

"Good-day... This is our teacher... Perhaps before everyone assembles you could look at the school and reading-room. It's not too far away."

The fellow in the jacket looked at him askance, ran his grey eyes searchingly over Horobenko's face, and hesitantly offered his hand:

"Mykola Batiuk."

"Good, I'll gladly come along. Where do we go?"

Batiuk studied his face once more and coughed.

"Please, I'll show you the way."

"Well, you go then, while I stir things up in the Executive Committee office." Harasymenko said, turning back and making off in the direction of the square, slightly dragging his right foot. Against the green backdrop of the trees his deep red velour cap blazed like a large thistle in the sun.

Batiuk moved along in silence for a while, summoning the words to start a conversation. Occasionally he would drift away to one side and cast sideways glances at Horobenko, sizing him up.

He felt uneasy in the silence, wanting to say many things to this communist, who was a Ukrainian after all, but he did not know how to begin.

The way out was provided all of a sudden, when Horobenko felt an unpleasant twitch in his stomach and, forgetting himself, he whispered:

"Ah, to hell with it, I forgot to grab some bread."

Batiuk was relieved.

"You haven't had breakfast yet? Follow me then, please… This is my house here…"

His youthful, pimpled face immediately became naively sincere, making him look even younger. He no longer looked askance, his slightly crafty eyes looked straight ahead, and a smile lurked in their corners.

"We'll have some of our maize gruel…"

At the table Batiuk completely shed his timidity and aired countless complaints as they consumed the gruel.

"…It really is quite difficult here. The party cells are dominated by Russians, and even when there is one of ours like Harasymenko, they're Russifiers all the same."

Horobenko smiled involuntarily: Harasymenko – a Russifier! This really was funny. What kind of 'Russifier' could he be, when he couldn't string two Russian words together! He simply did not care about either language. He was totally committed to solving social problems.

But Batiuk did not agree with this:

"That may be true: he may be just as coarse as us all, however his politics are sometimes worse than those of an inveterate Russky. Take this for example: there was a pamphlet in the reading-room by Charlemagne titled *Protect Your Native Flora and Fauna*… I should add, by the way, that this Harasymenko checks through all the new books himself. Well, know what? Harasymenko confiscated the pamphlet."

Horobenko placed his spoon on his plate and peered at Batiuk in surprise.

"*Da, da*, he confiscated it! Said: what is this about 'native' flora and fauna? All flora and fauna are international. This is a nationalist-oriented publication. It should not be made available."

Horobenko burst out in loud laughter. Batiuk did not like the laughter. His concealed, timorous hostility was now surfacing.

"It may be something to chuckle about, but when you have to work with such 'activists' each day, it makes you want to cry sometimes. I don't understand: there are Ukrainians in the party, after all, why don't they do anything?"

Horobenko looked intently at Batiuk and his gaze passed right through the fellow's stout figure.

Batiuk let open the floodgates, he not only complained now, he also accused, reproached and ridiculed.

Horobenko stopped eating, folded his arms across his chest and listened without saying a word.

All this talk was actually nothing new to him. Hadn't he heard all this from Pedashenko, Kovhaniuk and all those other sectarians who comprised the miserly handful of 'conscious Ukrainians' in the district town! Those operetta-like characters with sentimentally romantic souls and sorrowfully sarcastic eyes, who in the blossoming of their zeal and pathos were only capable of creating 'Prosvita', this new temple built on the ruins of a Ukrainian Jerusalem…? None of this was new to him. They knew only how to complain and sigh: 'On our native, but foreign land'…

Well, yes. And this Batiuk was quoting these very words now, just like hundreds of others. He was one of many. An average representative of the Ukrainian intelligentsia. Admittedly, it was rural, but what other one was there? There was none. Those who had led the Haydamak[20] detachments, who had filled the Ukrainian National Republic's ministries, travelling on diplomatic missions to represent Ukraine – they were different. The

---

20   The Haydamaks were volunteer units formed in response to the Bolshevik threat to Ukraine in December 1917.

quintessence. Equivalent to those who were lurking in the forests with sawn-off rifles.

The Batiuks were not of this calibre. All they could do was complain. Maybe even furtively, in quiet corners, hissing at those like Harasymenko. At Shevchenko's anniversary they would announce at school that Shevchenko was a revolutionary, that he had fought against Muscovite (they would emphasize this point) aristocracy, that he loved Ukraine… And with these dispirited words they would smuggle through a disguised nationalism, satisfied that it had turned out both Red and national in its orientation…

They were the eternal servants of God and Mammon.

Batiuk's doleful, primitive words, his face red with emotion and pimples, and his soiled embroidered shirt with its blue button under his jacket irritated Horobenko. 'What insolence they have…! These pimple-faced rural teachers, who are incapable of any act, forever being servile, these small people who through the ages have borne anaemia and treachery in their blood, they still thought about creating a state! Having nothing more behind them than sentimental sorrow and mouldy 'sacred national relics', they could still complain! They still wanted the authorities to hear them? The authority of those who bought their right to exist with blood and the suffering of tortured souls on countless fronts? No, this was at the very least naive!'

Horobenko felt disgust awaken and stir within him. He moved away from the table a little and tried not to look at Batiuk… Now, a bandit, that was another matter. He was a savage, inveterate enemy. And he was active. He had to be mercilessly fought, but he could still be made sense of. While these people… They were eternal enemies. This might seem paradoxical, but it was true: savage actions, wild temperament and fury were all probably more to the point than their indifferent coldness. Even from purely national interests these Batiuks needed to be shot dead, for a young nation could not be sentimentally rotten, infected with pustules…! It had to be made of iron.

And once more a paradoxical thought occurred to Horobenko:

The new, young Ukraine would be composed of others. Not these people. But those like Harasymenko. Those same Harasymenkos who were now throwing out Ukrainian books because of the word 'native', who crippled their speech by selecting new, strange words for those notions which had uprooted their lives and pushed them from their well-trodden ancestral path. Yes, the new Ukrainian nation would be composed of Harasymenkos. And this wasn't even a paradox, if only in fact national consciousness was not an invention, an illusion, but a totally real thing. If there was something biological behind it.

Actually, was it biological or economical? Batiuk would not allow Horobenko to think through his thoughts. He wiped his chin with a towel and sighed:

"This is our historical fate: we are being swindled and we don't even notice it."

This time Horobenko looked Batiuk in the eye with an openly hostile stare.

He itched to scream: 'You're a bitter nationalist! I'm going to arrest you…!'

But instead Horobenko screamed nothing of the sort. He only said dryly:

"You don't understand the historical process of social struggle. Take me to the reading-room. Where is it?"

They moved briskly down the street in the fresh morning air without exchanging a word. Batiuk walked a short distance behind him. He looked dejectedly at the dust kicked up by Horobenko's feet and was obviously suffering. The snubbed candour and meek shadow of their intimacy had been left behind in his home, by the plate of maize gruel, and here, when something needed to be said to this now reticent, unfathomable Ukrainian Communist, he could find no words. Batiuk picked at his brain, but all the words, which surfaced were not the ones he needed. And yet with every step that took them further from his house he realized that he badly needed to say something. After all, he had to unravel that remark: 'You don't understand the historical process of social struggle.'

The reading-room was already in view, and Slavina and Druzhynin were hurrying to join them, when Batiuk finally plucked up the courage. He stopped, and in confused fear, blinking, mumbled quietly;

"You must forgive me… I obviously had no desire to offend you, comrade. I spoke to you from the heart, as a Ukrainian…"

Horobenko replied in a cold, distant voice:

"I'm a communist, comrade."

Slavina drew up to them at a trot, threatening him coquettishly with her hand.

"What's this? You went off without saying a word! We barely managed to catch up to you… Off to the reading-room? Let's go."

Druzhynin was waiting for them on the porch.

The reading-room was impressive with its neatness and order. Announcements, posters, portraits of Shevchenko, Franko, Drahomanov – all this had been assiduously nailed up, adorned with embroidered sashes and branches of greenery.

A large red canvas in the middle immediately caught one's eye with the words: 'Through the national to the international!'

The tattered books and some newspapers were neatly stored in a cupboard.

Batiuk stood downcast by the door. He looked so forlorn and miserable, as if these three communists, who had come to inspect the reading-room out of curiosity, had broken into a kulak house to requisition chests acquired over the years and to empty the grain bins, and he was the owner. Batiuk watched Horobenko and Slavina askance, but their praises seemed not to reach his ears.

Slavina ran about the reading-room like a hen, poking her nose everywhere, as if pecking seeds:

"The portraits have been nicely adorned. But why are there none of Ilyich? I'll definitely send you one from town…"

Druzhynin tarried for a long time in the furthest corner, examining something on the wall. At last he turned around and asked Horobenko feebly:

"So Mazepa[21] was a revolutionary too?"

Something gave a jab inside Horobenko. He came up to Druzhynin, anxious.

"No, of course not. Why, what's the matter?"

Druzhynin turned away calmly to face the wall:

"He's on the wall here. I wasn't sure. I thought hetmans were like our tsars."

Dressed in a gold-embroidered mantle, Mazepa's face appeared young and majestic on the wall, framed in oak.

Horobenko flushed crimson for no reason at all. This Mazepa seemed to be hung here by his own hand, not Batiuk's. And now he had been caught on slippery ground. For some reason he solicitously read the inscription on

---

21   Ivan Mazepa was a firm supporter of a pan-Ukrainian state who opposed Russia's domination of Ukraine and attempted to win freedom for Ukraine by siding with the Swedes against the Russian tsar.

the portrait, then turned sharply to face Batiuk and called out irritably in a raised, superior voice:

"I really think, comrade teacher, that you could have found something more appropriate to hang here, instead of this Petliurite rubbish…!"

Slavina became rooted to the spot and fearfully opened her mouth.

The stairs outside creaked under Harasymenko's heavy boots.

XIII

Even before the start of the meeting the overcrowded school was filled with the heavy breathing of sweat-soaked bodies. A black mass of bearded human flesh surrounded the presidium table on three sides and weighed down on Horobenko with its uncombed, grubby enormity. One's eyes could not escape it. Except perhaps by looking at the ceiling, but even there, in the home-grown tobacco smoke and vapours, the drunken wheezing spirit of this mass of humanity was beating convulsively against the blackened whitewash of the walls.

This grey mash of peasant rags had flooded the large classroom and lapped threateningly at one's very feet. The ninth wave would strike at any moment and smash the tables, the benches, crushing the unfortunate re-election troika and the party cell in one fell swoop, flooding the villages, roads and forests with torrid insurrection…

The assembly of Soviets was only about to begin, but a hostile mood was already darting about the room like a snake, hissing ominously from the back, where faces merged into a single wrinkled stain.

Harasymenko stood at the side of the table, solemn and stern. He studied the long, entangled rows of people and a shadow settled on his forehead.

Without turning around, he addressed Horobenko, speaking almost under his breath:

"*Da*, there'll be trouble with the rich ones. They're provoking the crowd already."

A calm Druzhynin and silent, taciturn Slavina were sitting at the table. She was irritated and angered by the unceremonious, inquisitive and slightly derisive stares of the peasant men. Many wide-open eyes had become fixed on her, examining every spot on her, as if she was some circus freak.

Druzhynin sucked on his cigarette and looked wearily into the crowd. Harasymenko tinkled a small school bell, but its clanging only reached the front rows, swallowed up in the stormy hubbub of the room. It made no impression on those at the back.

Harasymenko desperately waved the bell over his head and shouted something. It was his waving hand, which probably quietened down the crowd, until it finally became silent. The middle and back rows pricked up their ears. Horobenko stood up, and it suddenly became far too quiet in the classroom.

He was even a little awestruck by the guarded, thick silence and Harasymenko's stern, solemn figure seemed so small and helpless.

Horobenko had prepared himself for a background of human voices, and so his voice now rang out, needlessly high-pitched and piercing:

"In the name of the re-election troika I pronounce the Fedorivka Rural District Congress of Soviets open...

"Comrade villagers! You have gathered here today as the masters of your rural district, to solve the burning issues of your life. Our congress is taking place under unusual circumstances. Our glorious Red Army has pushed the Polish aristocracy back across the

Dnipro River and Budenny's invincible cavalry is charging toward the palaces of Warsaw..."

As was customary in such instances in town, Slavina began to clap energetically. The crowd transferred its surprised eyes to her, and the presidium became dis-concerted. Slavina blushed in embarrassment but continued to clap even more enthusiastically. Druzhynin joined in, then Harasymenko began pounding his strong palms together. Those in the front row closest to the table hesitantly made a few confused noiseless claps and then Horobenko continued in his loud voice.

It was an ordinary speech with pathetic expressions alien to the coarse peasant mind, but this was only a beginning. This was only the foundation, which would break through the sand to the firmament beneath and then a solid wall would be raised upon it.

Hundreds of intent eyes watched Horobenko, catching his every word, his every move. They really seemed to be listening with their eyes and not their ears. Each word that he uttered swung the scales of their mood. Everything, which would follow depended on his speech. After all, the bearded body of people, which had filled the classroom and made the air stifling might not let them out of here. Horobenko was unable to connect with their eyes – they melted into dashes, commas, blurred contours – but he could intuitively sense the hostile looks, which pierced his face from every direction. Horobenko knew in his heart that this was the same crowd, which had passed through the whole of human history with shouts of 'Crucify him!'

Horobenko's nerves tensed like the string of a cross-bow, and his will to overcome the crowd grew, he wanted to defeat it. More than anything else he wanted to over-power it! He drifted away from tired, hackneyed, official terms and hit at the crowd with his own words, which flowed from some secret inner source, from his heart, generated by his nervous tension.

The crowd remained deadly silent. There was not even any wheezing or creaking of footwear. Horobenko could only sense the hundreds of heads craning toward him, catching and devouring his every word.

Was this crowd sympathetic or disaffected? It did not matter. The important thing was that it had already encircled him, it had unlocked the heavy bolts of its interior with Horobenko's words, and the initiative for action was now in Horobenko's hands.

"Long live Soviet power, the power of the workers and the peasants throughout the world…"

Exhausted, dripping with sweat, Horobenko returned to his chair with a slight tremor on his temple, while the rows stirred and applauded.

"I propose we sing *The Internationale.*"

Harasymenko had risen to his feet and announced this in broken Russian. Benches creaked in unison from all sides and several people began hesitantly in a hoarse, prayer-like voice, unaccustomed to the melody:

"Arise ye, wretched of the Earth…"

After the final refrain reached the open windows and dissolved somewhere in the street outside, followed, as usual, by an awkward silence, a cunning older voice called out from the crowd:

"Comrades, allow me to ask you a question…"

All heads turned around and at the end of what seemed like a passage appeared a pair of piercing eyes with a thin, flock-like beard. A bony, talon-like hand tugged at this beard, as if picking through the individual hairs.

"As the comrade from the city just told us, we are in control here, and indeed that is so, only we would like to…"

Harasymenko rose anxiously to his feet and looked sharply at the bearded fellow. His clenched fist softly drummed the tabletop. He seemed keen to say something, while the fellow shrunk back a little under his gaze, but continued:

"So that, of course, this matter can be placed on a more businesslike footing, we would like to sing the Lord's Prayer…" The fellow turned around and scooped at the air with his hand holding a hat. "So, am I right or not? I've finished…"

A wave of agreement spread through the back rows: "He's right! The Lord's Prayer! That's what we want!"

Slavina giggled hysterically, but her mirth was quashed by a roar which exploded somewhere near the far wall and was already engulfing the middle rows.

Harasymenko slammed his fist down on the table and for a moment his voice rose above the din:

"No paternosters here! The kulak scum are staging a provocation…"

But his last words were drowned by a fresh, savage, even louder outburst:

"The Lord's Prayer…!"

"So, the devil's 'national' is permitted, but not prayers…!"

"…Skrypnychenko, you begin…"

"Toss the sons of bitches out the window…!"

The crowd was working into a frenzy. Before his eyes Horobenko saw flashes of hands, twisted lips, someone's thrust-out chest. On one side he could already hear a furtive:

"Our Father, who art in Heaven…"

Horobenko rose sharply to his feet and raised his hand high. The crowd immediately became silent and the singing broke off. Druzhynin was tugging at his left sleeve:

"Let me speak to them… They'll understand…"

Horobenko called out sharply:

"The worker (he clearly emphasized the word) Comrade Druzhynin has the floor."

A whisper spread through the crowd and died away. Calmly, without hurrying, Druzhynin left his seat and moved in front of the table.

"Comrades, *radiany*...!" At first Horobenko was puzzled by this form of address, but then he understood: though speaking in Russian, Druzhynin wanted to adapt his language to the specific rural conditions, and this *radiany* of his was a combination of two Ukrainian words which he knew: *rada* – council or Soviet, and *hromadiany* – citizens.

"The point, *radiany*, is not that it's the Lord's Prayer. Who is forbidding that? Go ahead! But for that there's the church..."

Druzhynin's gaunt, sallow working-class face had an effect on the assembled people. His poise and calm were passed on to the crowd. The crowd cooled down and grew silent. No one had any objections and Horobenko suggested they elect a congress presidium.

"How shall we elect it, comrades, by a list or individually?"

And again, the wall behind the crowd answered with an importunate and stubborn roar:

"Individually! Individually!"

A second time the room filled with a racket and the school resounded to shouts of:

"Endeevidually!"

"No lists!"

"We don't understand what this 'endeevidually' means."

"No lists! There's no need for them"

Nearby a voice said: "We request that lists be used! The Party cell proposes the following list..." but it was swallowed up by the roar of the crowd.

Harasymenko became sullen and pale.

"I told you there'd be a problem with the rich. They've already incited the people…"

Horobenko raised his hand and, just like the first time, the commotion immediately subsided.

"All right. We'll do it individually. Please make your nominations."

Once more the wave burst forth, once more the fiery steed of the crowd broke its bridle:

"Pokotylo! Pokotylo…! Sydorenko…! Pavliy… We want Pokotylo…!"

Someone's booming voice called out:

"Teacher Batiuk, Mykolay Fedorovych!"

As if conspiring, the crowd roared in unison:

"Yes, the teacher! The teacher…! Mykolay Fedoro-vych!"

Batiuk stood by the door, smiling.

The smile was like finely crushed glass in Horoben-ko's eyes and scratched at his lungs. Aha, so that's it! In a united front, chaps? I should have expected as much. But no, to hell with you a hundred times! I won't let this happen! No!

However, the reins of the meeting were already being snatched from Horobenko's hands.

Batiuk stepped up to the table and, without asking for the floor, simply addressed the congress:

"Respected community! I thank you for the honour, but I cannot accept. I have the school, the reading-room, and a family…"

The crowd blustered even louder than before:

"We want Mykolay Fedorovych! Mykolay Fedorovych!"

Horobenko rushed out from behind the table and yelled at the top of his voice: "Keep quiet, Citizen Batiuk! Resume your place!"

The people in the front rows became silent from the yelling, those at the back followed suit. Batiuk stepped aside in fright, but immediately afterwards smiled again. Horobenko took a deep breath of the stifling, dirty air and addressed the crowd in a sharp tone:

"As the head of the re-election troika I forbid the candidacy of teacher Batiuk! This is no place for disguised Petliurite sentiments…!"

After these words Horobenko finally lost any control he might have had over the meeting. The room was swallowed up in a passionate lament.

It became impossible now to tell who was shouting what. To add to this, several dry shots sounded in the distance from the village outskirts and the sound of horses' hooves could be heard outside the school.

The classroom was bursting with a frenzy of confusion. And in this hell Horobenko suddenly sensed a passionate and fervent death. It breathed like hot coals at him from the contorted sweaty bodies and had already stretched its hand out toward the presidium. Any moment now it would have the final say and then something terrible would happen.

Harasymenko hastily removed his pistol from its holster and pointed it before him. Slavina let out a shriek and backed into a corner. Filled with horror, her eyes were riveted on Harasymenko's pistol.

But a strange thing happened: the crowd suddenly became silent, shrank back and wilted. A live path was cut through the crowd and along it hurried Popelnachenko and Drobot, accompanied by three Red Army soldiers, all of them armed.

Popelnachenko clenched the strap of his rifle and whispered into Horobenko's ear:

"Let's get the hell out of here, immediately. There's a gang entering the village."

A few more shots echoed outside again, this time much closer.

Popelnachenko turned sharply to face the meeting:

"The congress is being adjourned. A Revolutionary Committee will be appointed here. But remember – if anyone so much as lifts a finger to help the gang…"

He didn't finish. A blaze of gunfire erupted nearby. A windowpane tinkled merrily, and broken glass crashed onto the sill.

The crowd rushed away from the windows and gushed in a torrent toward the door.

"Stop! Mother of God…!"

Drobot jumped up onto a bench and raised his hand, holding aloft a coniform Austrian bomb.

"No one make a move!"

The crowd froze. The Red Army soldiers cocked their rifles. Popelnachenko took a step forward and ordered calmly:

"Communists, follow me!"

Outside there was a feverish exchange of gunfire right next to the school.

XIV

"I guess we can begin the meeting?"

Like a saint on an icon, Khanov placed his hands before him on the table and surveyed those present.

Makaron nodded in agreement, looking phlegmatically at an inkstand. Gander wriggled nervously in his chair, stretched his neck upwards, as if his collar was troubling him, and sneaked glances at Horobenko. Borysenko sunk back into an armchair and was strangely silent.

The 'staff room' was much too restless. Something prevented the pedagogues from beginning to chew on their usual mollified phrases, to feebly drawl about the state of instruction at the teachers' courses. Each of them imagined only too well the absurdity and futility of speaking now on an empty stomach about some new educational plan, seeking new approaches, when there was nothing to eat, no textbooks, no notebooks or even pens. Each of them appraised their participation in meetings and conferences as a game of cheat, however when they assembled, they pretended to be working, pondering and searching. This never worked for them though, because they merely wanted to learn about their rations, the latest fresh rumours and to quickly scurry off home to their gardens to plant cucumbers and potatoes. For this reason, the pedagogues never lingered at meetings…

However, on this day the meeting was not to their liking.

Khanov supported his temples with his fingers, cast his eyes over his glasses and addressed his colleagues again.

"Well, perhaps we can begin?"

Borysenko hastily jumped to his feet, as if stung, and measured out the 'staff room' with a nervous step.

"Actually, I first wanted to ask…" Borysenko paused and looked Horobenko in the eye. "*Da*… yes, I wanted to ask whether my respected colleagues consider it…" Borysenko faltered, stroked his pointed beard, and said with emphasis, "*normal* for the lecturer of Ukrainian, Comrade Horobenko, to allow himself to report secretly about what we discuss here…?"

Horobenko forced a smile, but immediately felt his cheeks flush red and the air became stifling.

Gander hissed maliciously in the silence: "*Da-a*…"

"Viktor Semenovych, perhaps we could postpone the matter…?" the alarmed Khanov tried to defuse the incident, which hung threateningly over the 'teacher's room', but Gander firmly objected in Russian:

"*Nyet*, how can we? It's impossible… This concerns us all, we can't…"

Makaron gave Horobenko an indifferent look with his cold, micaceous eyes and champed away noiselessly.

Horobenko crossed his legs and tried to bear up to Borysenko's stare. He even mumbled mutely:

"Well, well… please…"

This angered Borysenko. He turned to the pedagogues and sang out in a melodramatic languid baritone:

"I'm asking whether we can agree to be spied upon, to be informed on?!"

Gander ground his chair into the floor:

"It's simply vile…!" he said in Russian.

Horobenko rose and stretched out a hand toward Khanov:

"I'd like a word."

Borysenko sat down and raised his head disdainfully:

"Precisely. Please explain yourself to us, Comrade Horobenko!" he continued in Russian.

Gander raised an eyebrow at Makaron:

"Interesting indeed…"

Khanov once again wriggled anxiously in his chair, not knowing where to bury his eyes:

"Comrades, perhaps we can settle this matter somehow…"

But Horobenko had already moved away and grabbed the back of his chair firmly with his hands.

"Well then, please. I don't, of course, intend to justify myself here, I just wanted to say…"

Gander flinched and hastily interrupted in Russian:

"It seems to me that it's somewhat inconvenient for a lecturer of Ukrainian to speak Ukrainian here… Since we don't understand…"

Khanov stood up and drummed his fingers impatiently on the table said in Russian:

"Excuse me, Nikolay Ivanovich, in our republic each citizen can speak his own tongue… Besides, we do live in Ukraine…"

Horobenko shuddered and pressed his lips tightly together. Khanov awaited his words with horror. Horobenko waited for a minute, rubbed his cheek and heavily ran his eyes about the room, as if this had been his first time here.

"Ye-e-es… It's very good that we've come to an understanding… Now everything is clear…"

The 'staff room' sank into a tense silence. And then Horobenko exploded with unprecedented force:

"There is real counter-revolution ensconced here!"

The pedagogues flinched and froze. Horobenko lashed out again:

"I intend to take steps to scatter this clique… Enough is enough!"

Khanov jumped from his place and stretched his hands out to Horobenko, pleading:

"I beg your pardon! Konstantin Petrovich! Why this? My dear fellow, this is an obvious misunderstanding…"

Pale-faced, Gander hastily pattered over to Horobenko on his short, bandy legs:

"No, Comrade Horobenko… allow me… you completely misunderstood… I in no way wanted to…" he gabbled away in Russian.

Horobenko tossed his hair back and then said in a triumphant drawl:

"I've finished. I have nothing further to add. There's only work left for the Cheka here…"

Horobenko turned sharply and left the room. The 'staff room' froze, as if in the last scene of Gogol's *The Inspector General.*

One last time Horobenko pushed open the spring-loaded front door of his former high school and it crashed shut behind him loudly and ungraciously.

'Yes, I'm finished here. There's no middle line nor can there ever be! I'll write an appropriate report tonight and hand it over to Zivert for the Cheka…'

Horobenko walked briskly along the deserted noonday streets, still feeling light-hearted, and hurried away from the pedagogical technical school.

"Yes, yes… Such a fine lot! Really! Well, they've finally blabbed their fill. And what impudence! What certainty, to hell with them…! Ah, it was crystal clear: though Horobenko was a communist, he was an intellectual all the same. Where had anyone seen an intellectual snitch on others! He was treated like one of them, as a 'decent fellow'! Ah, the scum! 'Decent fellow'? I'll show you 'decent'! Yes, yes, I'll personally write to the Cheka today, precisely the Cheka!"

Popelnachenko was right when he had said that Horobenko needed to be sent three or so times to deal with the kulaks before the intellectual would be shaken out of him.

'Only you were wrong, Popynaka – once was enough… That trip with the re-election troika was enough to set me against them. Was it not symbolic then that Popelnachenko should have saved me from the gang and the delirious peasants back then? The gang, and the old peasants, and Batiuk – they were 'our people', Ukrainians! They were 'for Ukraine'. And these damned beadles – they were on the other side too, but they were different enemies, enemies of both Ukraine and the revolution… Ah, why can't Popynaka and Krycheyev,

and the rest of them not understand that in Ukraine the matter of nationality is so closely bound to the social question…? Why won't they understand that the Ukrainian national question is a completely real, vital notion, and not some mere fantasy…? But then – no, the time will come, and they will understand. It has to be so. It can't be any other way!

All this is leading to something better. Both that Party Committee character reference in my file and the suspicion with which they regard me – all this is for the better. You are no longer the same person, Horobenko. No, no, not the same person. The Rubicon has been crossed. And there is no turning back. There are only extreme measures. There is no middle road. There or there. Don't evade things which pain you, the complicated and the incomprehensible. That is the way of the intelligentsia.

Grab hold of it by the roots and hack into it. Simplify all those damned questions to an axiom, to $2 \times 2 = 4$. Shoot down all intellectual prejudices in you with machine-gun laughter, prejudices, which were once nurtured, but now are only an encumbrance. To hell with this millwheel around your neck, which only drags you down into the pit of counter-revolution. Yes, Horobenko – counter-revolution! Because now there is revolution or counter… without an intellectual middle road. So, uproot this rubbish and toss it onto the refuse heap, along with all those Batiuks, Husaks and Borysenkos.'

These thoughts raced through his mind with centrifugal speed, intoxicating his brain, headily blurring his outlook. And suddenly at the very centre of it all there appeared a wavering, naive, almost childish question:

"Is this you, Kostyk? Can it really be you…?"

Kost Horobenko replied joyously to this inner voice, as if it was that of an idiotic, long familiar fool:

"Yes, yes, don't be amazed my friend – it is me. Actually, not me, but that which was once me. Kostyk has died, or, to be truthful, he has been dying gradually, and that which has not yet died will in any case soon be dead. But then, what is death? I'm not a philosopher, but even without philosophy it is evident, without much thought, that the death of one is at the same time the birth of another. Therefore, death is unable to interrupt the eternal kaleidoscope of life…! Do you understand any of this, my friend? It's so simple and clear. You must realize that Kostyk no longer exists, just like there is no more Nadia, no father with his two buildings, nothing of what existed then. Now there is 'Comrade Horobenko'. A member of the CP(b)U. Understand what a beautiful life this is, the devil take it! How beautiful it is…! And I thank the Revolution, I thank the Party for teaching me to love it so fondly."

XV

Druzhynin seated himself down on the chair in front of Krycheyev's desk and tapped the hole punch against his filer.

"Comrade Krycheyev, none of those Marxisms can justify simple human inanity! There's no need to tell me stories...!"

Krycheyev smiled faintly and twirled the pencil in his fingers. Druzhynin turned away from Krycheyev, offended, and addressed Popelnachenko:

"This is great! I'm walking past our theatre this morning, when I stop and hear hammering coming from the roof above. What's going on? I thought perhaps Radchenko had found a way to repair the theatre. I looked up, but they were ripping the iron sheeting off the roof, the sons of bitches.

"Do you follow me, Popynaka?"

Popelnachenko smiled and coughed:

"No, so far I don't understand a damned thing."

"Well, get this brother, this in fact is our attempt at construction. Radchenko is reforming it. The idiot ordered the theatre to be dismantled and cinematographic booths to be built on the outskirts of town from its bricks and iron sheeting! His head's not screwed on right, brother!"

Popelnachenko drew closer to Druzhynin and slapped him on the knee:

"Don't beat about the bush, Druzhynin. Something isn't right here. So, you'd better tell me…"

Druzhynin became indignant:

"What do you mean, 'not right'? I went myself to ask Radchenko."

"And?"

"Here's your 'and'! He says, what other alternative can there be? The theatre is centrally located, it will always be at the service of the bourgeoisie, it needs to be moved closer to the masses. Lenin said: cinema is the best way of educating the proletariat, well then, sacrifice the bricks from the theatre for the cinematographic booths. That's what he's cooked up, brother!"

Krycheyev was surprised and did not want to believe him:

"You're exaggerating, it couldn't have been like that."

"It's a fact! A whole cartload of tin sheeting has already been carted off to the Svynarka district... I even asked him: 'Comrade Radchenko, what if I or anyone of our members wanted to take his wife and kids to the theatre – then is that also 'theatre at the service of the bourgeoisie'?"

Druzhynin spat on the ground and shook his head:

"No, my dear comrades, this is no way to behave...!"

Party committee members stood around him and smiled. No one seriously believed that such an outlandish plan of reconstruction could really have entered Radchenko's head. For this reason, they failed to comprehend why Druzhynin had seized on the theatre so passionately. All this seemed more like an anecdote to them, than something from real life, and their outbursts of laughter and jokes gradually shifted from the nature of the incident to Druzhynin himself, his animation and gesticulation.

But Druzhynin would not calm down. He was pained and fervently defended the old tumbledown building of the town theatre, stranded next to a putrid stream under the willows; it was as if they were discussing the ruin of his own ancestral home.

"...Lenin said that 'film is a good thing' – correct. But you must understand, you blockhead, what it means and where to apply it. If you are given power, you idiot, then use it wisely, instead of performing circus tricks..."

Horobenko listened to Druzhynin from afar and marvelled at him. He liked both Druzhynin's frank indignation and his frank candour, and the fact that this outburst was directed at Radchenko (that meant that finally Radchenko would be exposed!).

Druzhynin was a small, contemporary sketch of the future proletariat. The whole proletariat would one day be like him. Druzhynin had now come to the rescue of the theatre, which had been quite alien to him. What had it given him? Former 'Little Russian' plays, 'Prosvita' concerts and *The Bayadere*. Still, Druzhynin wanted to save the theatre, trying to rescue it from Radchenko's experiments. Therefore, art too, the abstract art of tomorrow and the putrid art of today, was not at all alien to him. Eh, you nice, kind Druzhynin...!

Krycheyev finally put an end to the conversation:

"I'll investigate this matter further, Comrade Druzhynin. Comrade Birynberg, summon Radchenko tomorrow for four o'clock. And now..." Krycheyev made himself more comfortable in his armchair, "let's begin our meeting. Today we have a talk by the chairman of the State Publishing House branch. Comrade Miliutin – the floor is yours."

The Party members reluctantly drifted away from Druzhynin and scattered throughout the room.

The rotund Miliutin monotonously and indifferently drawled out endless figures about books and magazines received from the centre and again pulled out new

BORYS ANTONENKO-DAVYDOVYCH

ribbons of figures on the dissemination of literature in the outlying districts. Each of those present seemed to be thinking their own thoughts and no one listened to Miliutin. Only Popelnachenko, his elbows resting on his knees, looked askance at Miliutin's tiny grey flattened eyes and Krycheyev occasionally jotted something in his notebook.

After Miliutin had finished, Popelnachenko was the first to seek the floor with a question:

"I would like to know why the State Publishing House branch is disseminating portraits of Drahomanov and where they obtained them from?"

Miliutin's eyes darted about guiltily:

"It actually isn't the branch's doing… From memory, Comrade Horobenko brought them to us from the former 'Prosvita', or something like that, and we…"

Popelnachenko twisted his lips sarcastically and smiled. Those present transferred their weary gazes in surprise to Horobenko. Once more Horobenko felt his heart pound away uneasily and his cheeks turned stupidly red. He stretched his hand toward Krycheyev:

"May I have the floor… Yes, it was I who handed the State Publishing House branch the portraits of Drahomanov. As you are aware, Drahomanov is an old Ukrainian revolutionary. I see nothing criminal in my actions…"

Horobenko wanted to return Popelnachenko's sarcastic smile, but it turned out far too miserly. Near Krycheyev the district supply commissar, Drobot, was asking someone in a deep voice:

"Who's this Drahomanov? I don't seem to recall his name…"

Popelnachenko rose to his feet and smiled malevolently. Then his face became serious and the yellow bloodless skin bulged out on his cheekbones, shining:

"Comrades! I declare that Drahomanov is a well-known Ukrainian nationalist. These portraits must be removed from all reading-rooms and schools. And Horobenko needs to be grabbed firmly by the snout…"

Everyone stared in silence at Horobenko, as if he had just been convicted. Horobenko moved hastily up to Krycheyev.

"I protest at such gross misrepresentation. In the end we can refer the matter to the centre, since Comrade Popelnachenko doesn't know himself…"

Once more Popelnachenko declared firmly:

"I propose the portraits be removed."

Krycheyev stopped him.

"Popelnachenko, no need to get hot under the collar. We won't be settling the matter now. I'll think it over myself. Comrades, are there any more questions with regards to the speech?"

* * *

That day Horobenko did not go to the Communist Dining Hall, but instead went straight home along back streets and climbed into bed.

Once more he felt broken inside and his small room nestled abandoned somewhere in the very deepest pit of life.

Horobenko buried his face in a pillow and covered his head with his jacket. He shut his eyes tightly, pressing his hot hands between the knees of his drawn-up legs. But it was no use, Popynaka's twisted face was still before him and his ears reverberated to the words 'this is a well-known Ukrainian nationalist'…

The calm he had felt after his trip to the village and the scene with the pedagogues had passed. It had been completely annihilated and could never be restored.

'So, nothing has changed about the way they feel toward me. They still distrust me as before, to them I'm as much a nationalist as that Drahomanov.'

Again, his heart ached deep inside and stopped him from lying still in one spot. Horobenko turned over and thought in despair:

'All right then, if they consider me a Ukrainian nationalist, why don't they turf me out of the Party? That would be logical…'

Horobenko pushed the jacket away from his head and the gloomy soiled wall posed him a question:

"What would you do outside the Party…?"

Fool! What are you asking? Your bridges have long been burnt, and there is nothing for you to do outside the Party. Understand, there is nothing for you to do. Beyond the Party there is only a desert.

It makes no difference what they think of you. What's important is what you think about yourself. Do you really know yourself? You are no longer the fellow you once were, Horobenko. No, no – not at all. You know the importance of certain things. But who are you? Have a good think first – have you purged everything, which does not relate to communism, which flits about inside you from your past? Why the hell did you need Drahomanov, who although he is a Ukrainian revolutionary, was a Ukrainian all the same? And what does Drahomanov's Ukrainian ethos stand for in mankind's universal conflagrations, in that great fire which will sweep the earth in preparation for a new life! Well then, Horobenko? Speak up…!

Aha, Horobenko, so now you remember? That's just it!

The Central Rada.[22] Teachers, 'Cossack' soldiers and other party intelligentsia... And suddenly some bishop arrived before the white bastions of the Pedagogical Museum, claiming to be Ukrainian. He said a few words in broken Ukrainian and blessed the place. And what happened? The naive 'topknots'[23] went mad with joy. 'We have a bishop too! We are a real nation, we're not just peasants and teachers!'

You're like them, Horobenko, but from the opposite pole:

"We Ukrainians had revolutionaries too! Drahomanov, for example. Isn't the root of all this, the very essence, an embryo of nationalism? You want to emphasize that Drahomanov was a Ukrainian? Well, own up – isn't that true? Yes. Shouldn't it be all the same to a communist what nationality Drahomanov, Zhelyabov or Khalturin are? To a true communist, Kostyk, it is all the same. And Popelnachenko is right several times over, he even caught you at it today. Maybe he was wrong in his assessment of Drahomanov, he may have distorted the facts on purpose, but in the end Drahomanov was a revolutionary, maybe even a cosmopolitan (you know full well, Kostyk, that you don't even know Drahomanov all that well!), but you, Horobenko, whether you like it or not, are a Ukrainian nationalist after all, be it only one quarter, or an eighth, a tenth or even a hundredth part. You still haven't eradicated that from yourself. And besides, you're also a petty intellectual. That's what it is. That is the splinter sitting inside you, stopping you. They're quite right about you."

---

22   Literally, Central Council. It was set up in Kyiv on 17 March 1917 as an all-Ukrainian representative body, soon becoming the centre of the Ukrainian liberation movement.

23   *Khokhol* in Russian. A derogatory term used by Russians when referring to Ukrainians.

Horobenko slipped a hand under his head and tried to argue:

"But hold on! Aren't they proud of the fact that Lenin is a Russian, that Moscow has become the heart of world revolution? Don't they have that too?"

And once more the sullen unwhitewashed wall posed a question to him:

"Who are 'they'? After all, Popelnachenko is a Ukrainian by birth, so is Nestorenko, and Harasymenko too. While Drobot doesn't know himself who he is…"

The door was quietly opened by Paraska Fedotovna. She ran a furtive eye about the room and, convinced that there was no one else in the room, she entered quietly.

"I've come to you. You wouldn't like to taste some fresh patties, would you? Please. I've just baked them…"

Paraska Fedotovna placed the plate of patties on his table and sat down on the edge of the chair.

"…It's simply sweltering today! Working toward a fine storm. You've probably noticed, it's always like that – once it's humid during the day, there's a storm in the evening…"

Horobenko sat up in bed, lowered one foot to the floor and scowled.

"What did you say…? Patties…? Aha, patties, all right."

Paraska Fedotovna brought the plate up to him.

"Here, take one, please."

Horobenko lazily grabbed a patty, bit off a warm piece of it with some meat and suddenly sensed how terribly hungry he was. Greedily, without realizing it, he emptied the whole plate. Paraska Fedotovna smiled amiably at him.

"So, were they okay?"

Replying with a smile, Kost said childishly:

"They were delicious. Really delicious…"

He got up from the bed, stretched to his full height and involuntarily noticed Paraska Fedotovna's slightly sagging, but still firm breasts under her blouse. Paraska Fedotovna folded her hands on her knees and was tickling Horobenko merrily with an immodest, carnal gaze.

Horobenko paced across the room but could no longer help but return to the full-faced, stout woman with soft plump breasts. He turned around slowly and sensed even more distinctly how this mound of jiggling meat, reeking of cooking fat and onion, attracted him so irresistibly. Paraska Fedotovna gave a small wink with her left eye and said languidly:

"You must find it hard, being all alone…? How come you're on your own?"

Horobenko slid his hands in his pockets and approached Paraska Fedotovna with sweeping steps. His voice was hoarse and trembled a little:

"I *am* lonely, Paraska Fedotovna!" He involuntarily covered her broad shoulder with his hand and Paraska Fedotovna rested her tousled head against his belly.

Horobenko looked savagely at her naked shoulder and whispered subconsciously:

"Yes, I'm lonely, very lonely, to hell with it…!"

Paraska Fedotovna stroked his thigh and chuckled passionately:

"Ooh, my impetuous one! My wee little communist…"

*   *   *

How it had happened – Horobenko could still not work out. Flushed and bare-headed, Paraska Fedotovna lay on the bed beside him, stretching sweetly.

"Ooh, how impetuous you are…! Tired granny right out…"

BORYS ANTONENKO-DAVYDOVYCH

Horobenko looked with disgust at her corpulent bare knees, unable to tear his gaze from them. The wave of passion had passed like a cloudburst and he now felt slippery and dirty.

'Why doesn't she leave?' Horobenko thought irritably.

Taking her time, Paraska Fedotovna wiped herself with the hem of her soiled skirt and got up slowly.

"Well, now I have to go and feed the porker… Ho, ho, I'm exhausted…"

Paraska Fedotovna tied her hair into a knot at the back and sailed up to Horobenko. She paused before him for a minute, cocking her head as she admired him, and suddenly she hugged him and loudly smacked her lips against his cheek.

"My kind little communist…!"

This was so unexpected that Horobenko even drew back toward the wall. He looked with wide-open fearful eyes at the place where Paraska Fedotovna had been standing until a moment ago, and through the door he heard the echo of her slippers flopping away

down the passage.

The tortured bedding lay crumpled against the wall.

And once more a caressing, gentle voice spoke inside him. It was not reproachful, only melancholy:

'Is this you, Kostyk…?' And Nadia's live bust appeared near the window, two large transparent tears on her cheeks. Only two. There were never any more. This was the first and last time that Kost had seen them on Nadia's face as he hurried off from the warm evening twilight of Nadia's bedroom into the frost outside, into fields on his sad, unknown travels. That evening the Directory's detachments were leaving the city, that evening he saw Nadia alive for the last time. The last time…

Two tears. Two pure, limpid tears…

Suddenly his memory was invaded by the repugnant, vulgar dissonance of Paraska Fedotovna's shameless chuckling and her passionate utterance steeped in kitchen smells: 'My impetuous little communist!'...

Horobenko grabbed hold of his jaw, as if a tooth was suddenly troubling him, and limply collapsed into a corner.

And as a last reproach, a voice seeped deep into his chest and did not fade immediately:

"Woe is me! The best theories can coexist so simply and easily alongside the filthiest of practices..."

How ugly life was, after all...!

XVI

*   *   *

Kost had forgotten what he had seen before this. All that had suddenly plunged into oblivion, like the boring part of an uninteresting, insipid film. Instead the darkness divulged a short, surprisingly vivid, stunning fragment.

*   *   *

The first thing to register was the rhythmic clicking of military boots against the pavement.

"Hup! Hup…! Hup-two, hup-two…"

It was some military unit marching along. Perhaps a company, a battalion, or even a whole regiment. Only they weren't Red Army soldiers. No. They didn't march like this. These steps reflected nuts and bolts connected faultlessly to a well-tended, age-old mechanism.

Nothing would fly off here, there was only…

Click! Click! Hup-two, hup-two.

Iron heel plates had probably been nailed onto the heels of their boots and the boots themselves were a little too heavy, which was why they sounded like this.

But why were they wearing peakless caps? That was incomprehensible. Peakless caps had long since disappeared, but yet – where had he seen this picture?

Badly shorn heads, courageously wide-open eyes and frozen stony elbows supporting rifles resting on shoulders.

"Ah, how could I? Well, what kind of Red Army soldiers are these!?"

Kost strained his eyes and noted with horror the white cockades on the peakless caps and the chain on the red epaulettes.

"Eyes front! Draw up to the right… Gentlemen officers…" a voice rang out in Russian.

Kost looked harder and saw that the clicking against the pavement was in fact a crowd of richly dressed, festive people advancing toward him. Who were they? No, he couldn't make anything out. A white dress with a white bouquet of roses. Why such strange colour coordination – a white dress and large white roses? And anyway – why roses…? A priest's golden vestments, a police commissary with a silver sword-belt. Who was the commissary? Aha, it was Slatin! The same Slatin he had known from high school. And here were gold buttons on a blue tunic and the red ribbons of decorations. That looked like Khanov. What was his former aunt screaming, the one who had married the neophyte merchant? What was she doing here?

The thuribular chant of past litanies engulfed the street, the footpaths, the houses and the crowd. There were no more people. They had merged into a frenzied roar, in which the ear could barely discern the unpleasant, cracked reedy voice of the cathedral choirmaster, Suprunenko.

That damned, nauseously familiar singing drew closer and closer. Kost retreated and saw that he and the crowd were separated by a completely empty space. It grew smaller every instant.

Where was this? Was Denikin's army entering Kyiv or something…? Then why was his former aunt here, the one married to the convert, and the police commissary,

Slatin? And why were the buildings so low, and what was this old wooden bridge under the willows…? Ah, no. This was not Kyiv, this was his native district town, and here on the right was the putrid creek into which he had tossed the physicist's microscope.

Kost backed off and, without turning around had already stepped onto the rotten planks of the bridge, while the distance between him and the crowd kept getting smaller and smaller, catastrophically smaller. He needed to kick up his heels and run. Run without looking back. Without thinking. Get the hell out of here. Away from this devout roar and the sight of the crowd. But he didn't have the energy to run. He couldn't even turn around. The crowd had fixed its thousand-eyed gaze on him and was attaching him to itself, paralysing Kost. Kost was already at the far end of the bridge, while behind him the crowd had just reached the bridge. Both stopped unexpectedly.

Suddenly a swift wave surged through the crowd, an indecisive sharp movement, and then a Russian chant rose over the bridge, the willows, right up to the church domes: 'Beat the Jews and the commissars! The Jews…!'

Could Gander really have shouted that?! Would they really stoop so low…? And phlegmatic Makaron was moving alongside Slatin, stooped, holding a lasso…

Kost flinched. He became tense and: yes – he would not retreat now but decided to make straight for the crowd! He would come right up to its monstrous snout and, like a captured inveterate horse thief at a village lynching, would spit at the crowd:

"Here I am! Beat me up…!"

Kost had already moved his feet forward to take the first firm step when on his right he suddenly saw a small Jewish boy sitting peacefully on the bridge railing, thoughtlessly swinging his feet through the air. He was holding a small red flag and waving it joyously somewhere at the crows above, or the green treetops, or at the sun.

"Stupid little kid!" Kost exclaimed involuntarily. The boy had not seen the crowd and was smiling joyously. Kost wanted to call out to him to run away. But his jaws were locked tight and he couldn't utter a single word.

This unfortunate child would die, crushed by the savage crowd. Or it would fall headlong over the railing into the water. It could not be left there. The child and its small flag were all that remained of 'that', it was the last thing left between Kost and the crowd.

"Rescue him! Rescue the child!"

Kost strained every muscle and dashed off toward the boy, and at that very moment hooves sharply struck the opposite end of the bridge… jet-black horses… peakless caps… the sudden gleam of a sword…

*　　*　　*

Kost opened his eyes, sat up in bed and surveyed the room in amazement. A crumpled pillow hung off the bed and his blanket had fallen to the floor.

The wall was lightly painted with the dawn silhouettes of trees.

Kost dropped his feet to the floor, but still could not regain his senses.

"What a strange and exceptionally vivid dream…!"

A pale sunrise illuminated the window.

XVII

"Just a minute, Horobenko, I'll be with you presently."

Mysha Chernyshov moved his briefcase to one side, together with piles of 'cases', and immersed himself in the minutes. He pressed his palms against his temples, and this made his whitish hair ruffle up at the top, making Mysha Chernyshov appear like a poor helpless pupil unable to solve an exercise. These were all thrice-damned Judicial Section matters. With invisible saboteur's hands they ceaselessly wove an intricate lace of judicial definitions, from which one could never break free. Mysha Chernyshov had tried to wrest them apart, but nothing came of it. This was all very confusing, but it was complicated further still by Lawyer Terletsky.

Occasionally Mysha Chernyshov thought: why was it that Lawyer Terletsky had to hang around him all the time and waffle on? Why the hell did he need Terletsky with his Roman law and old statutes? Terletsky had a sow's lips and a white, browless face. At times Mysha Chernyshov looked at Terletsky and a thought immediately sprung to mind: what if they were to take one of these swinish mugs with its fleshy neck on which the fat collected in folds, shove a red egg into its mouth and place it in the window of the smallgoods shop...!

Then Mysha Chernyshov forgave Terletsky his petty-bourgeois background, the boring figures of the clauses with their endless points and looked mirthfully into his mouth. Without blinking an eye, Terletsky recounted anecdotes and adventures from his judicial practice, and Mysha Chernyshov listened to his witticisms, thinking: 'Obviously scum, but a man after all...'

However, Chernyshov understood perfectly: Terletsky was an awful blade and undoubtedly was deceiving him and the whole Judicial Section, hiding things from them. If the truth be known, Terletsky should have been done away with long ago.

But therein lay the tragedy: Terletsky – a saboteur and counter-revolutionary, who might even be accepting bribes from the kulaks – was nonetheless indispensable. And when some 'business' seemed quite a simple matter to Mysha Chernyshov, enabling one to grab the swindler by the gills and toss him to the wind without a second thought, Terletsky would calmly and peremptorily point to articles of various codes, falling back on VUTsVK[24] resolutions, People's Commissariat of Justice decrees, and in the end Mysha Chernyshov was forced to accede to his infinite black magic.

Because of Terletsky, like it or not, he had to pore over codes one more time, immerse himself in instructions and decrees and, without realizing it, lower himself into a clerical quagmire. This was quite an unnecessary bother and it angered him that Terletsky, without really dictating anything, was in fact dictating his actions and by his mere presence prompted Chernyshov, the director of the Judicial Section, to become bogged down in this bureaucratic red tape and paperwork.

"Just a minute... there's only a little more work here..." Chernyshov said hastily to Horobenko and knocked his knees together impatiently, attempting to comprehend the very essence of some protocol.

---

24 *VseUkrains'kyi Tsentral'nyi Vykonavchyi Komitet* – All-Ukrainian Central Executive Committee.

The door creaked open and half the courier's frail figure appeared, while behind him in the twilight of the passage lurked Terletsky's browless forehead and someone else's questioning, meek eyes.

The courier spoke in a high-pitched restless voice:

"Comrade Terletsky is here, he wants to see you. Is that all right? And there's also someone from Kupriyanivka…"

Without looking up, Mysha Chernyshov yelled out angrily:

"Give them all the boot…!"

Taking his time, the courier firmly closed the door, while Chernyshov mumbled with outrage in his voice:

"The buggers never let one finish reading…!"

Chernyshov had wanted to finish reading the protocol, but after the interruption he could no longer summon his scattered thoughts, being side-tracked by trifles. He tossed the protocol aside and waved his hand:

"Ah, to hell with it! I'll go over it tonight!"

He rose from his table and went over to a desk. He turned his key around twice in the drawer marked 'top secret' and sucked on a greenish bottle, like a child at its mother's breast. The liquid bubbled away merrily to his thirsty gulps and Mysha Chernyshov let out a satisfied groan.

"Listen, Chernyshov, what's this in aid of?" Horobenko asked gently and reproachfully.

"I can't otherwise, brother. The buggers would work me into a knot."

"But you're undermining your authority…"

"Come on, drop it! A fine professor you are to read me lectures!" Chernyshov barked back as he locked the drawer.

"Sooner or later they," Horobenko motioned toward the door with his eyes, "will find out about this…"

"What?!" Mysha Chernyshov turned sharply toward Horobenko. "I'll show the buggers how to 'find out'! I have my ways!"

Chernyshov described a complicated knot with sweeps of his hand and again lowered himself into his armchair.

"Well, to hell with them!" And Chernyshov immediately forgot about them all. "The point is this, Horobenko. I heard that you've organized an art workshop."

"That's right."

"You see, I have a young buddy. The sonofabitch draws really well! I wanted to send him to you, to get him to improve. By the way, how's the workshop coming along?"

"Send him along. The workshop…? It's still limping along. We lack funds."

Mysha Chernyshov asked seriously, with genuine interest:

"Do you have a teacher?"

"There's an instructor. A slovenly artist. The only problem we have is with nude models. We don't have any."

Mysha Chernyshov thought a while. He scowled a little, screwed up his eyes and suddenly brightened again:

"Know what, Horobenko, I've got an idea… I'll help you out. Brother, I've got two officer's wives steaming away in the DOPR,[25] sent there by the Cheka. They're good-for-nothing aristocrats – we could dispatch them to you as models…!"

Mysha Chernyshov turned red and rejoiced at his own resource-fulness. There was a gentle, naive twinkle in his

---

25 Russian acronym for *Dom prinuditel'nykh rabot*, House of Correctional Labour.

BORYS ANTONENKO-DAVYDOVYCH

eyes. But Horobenko grew sullen. As if not comprehending, he asked again:

"As nude models?"

Chernyshov leaned over enthusiastically toward Horobenko:

"Well, *da*! They're real cuties, see! One, Shyhoryna, is the wife of the cavalry captain… and the other one – man, oh man! No one's ever seen models the likes of these!"

Horobenko listened gloomily. Mysha's enthusiastic words circled like bats in his head, unable to settle down.

'Two officer's wives for models… Shyhoryna, the wife of the cavalry captain… steaming away in the DOPR… Naked female breasts… In the workshop…'

Horobenko shifted in his chair and asked in a stammer:

"But… maybe, this will be… I mean… hard for them…?"

Mysha Chernyshov was surprised, but then waved his hand about:

"What's so 'hard' about it? On the contrary. Besides, they're doing forced labour, so there's nothing to discuss…! You know, Shyhoryna isn't too hot, but Kanonova – she's… (Chernyshov paused to find a suitable simile) …It's as if she's stepped straight out of a painting! I've never seen a woman like her, oh brother…"

Horobenko's eyes grew large and he stared at Chernyshov in fright. Thoughts swirled around in his head, but Horobenko was unable to give them form.

…To take two women and, without asking their consent, just because they were captives, to force them to pose naked before his worker-soldier auditorium… That was much too brutal. It was even plain savage!

Eh you, Mysha Chernyshov! A small likeable, naive boy who played by slicing off a sick cat's tail with a blunt knife…!

And suddenly Kost thought:

'And what if Chernyshov had chosen Nadia just like that to become a model?'

An icy-cold lightning bolt shot down his back, but Horobenko roused himself, rose sharply, and said firmly:

"Good. Send the two officer's wives then. They'll come in handy... Come on, let's go. We must be late for the meeting already."

Horobenko turned abruptly and made for the door, while Mysha Chernyshov hastily stuffed documents into his briefcase.

XVIII

It was stuffy and smoky. The cheap tobacco smoke had shrouded the large hall in a blue haze and gave rise to a dull headache. The wiring was faulty and there was no electricity. Candles were burning. They burned solemnly, mysteriously and almost with a cautionary light. Moonlight struggled timidly through the opened windows on the right and became lost in the room. The large candles illuminated a few faces, carving deep wrinkles into them, fixing their expressions and, as if to compensate for this, the backs of people's heads became outlined even more darkly and shaggy silhouettes floated out of the darkness. The candles flickered quietly, and their flickering silently left its mark on the faces. The faces grew brighter, then darker. Someone was speaking. Ah, it was Zivert, the head of the Political Bureau. He was speaking, which was actually better this way—there would be no confusion with the district Cheka. But the silence of the candles was so oppressive, so solemn, that it seemed Zivert was not saying a thing. A large, mass pantomime was taking place. The sharp features of faces illuminated by the candles were brimming with sounds and their open lips were permeated with silence. For this reason, the Party organization's general meeting seemed conspiratorial, and Zivert's words were like a distant echo, exploding toward the ceiling and the windows, his resounding cries sounding almost prophetic.

"…There will be victims, there will be great losses. We must be prepared for this. The gangs have become much too insolent. They're even threatening the city now. Only the day before yesterday they tore to pieces the produce-allotment activists, Communist Kirpichnikov and Komsomol member Feihyn. We had to execute half the hostages in Zhuravne, but this will be repeated again and again. There's no need for kid gloves, comrades. The banditism must be burnt away with red-hot irons…!"

Zivert's gaunt face, with his protruding cheekbones and sunken cheeks, became lost and disappeared under his large, glistening eyes. The eyes swallowed up his face. The pallor of his face seemed to exist solely to frame in light grief the renunciation of everything irrelevant and the firm steadfastness, which burned in his eyes. Horobenko could not see Zivert's figure behind all the heads, he saw only a torso in a field jacket and the sweep of a hand gesturing with unrestrained determined movements, a steely dynamism.

The meeting had been going for four hours already, but there was no feeling of lassitude. What lassitude? Where was it? The squabbles had disappeared, the petty quarrels which had rustled through the organization – all this seemed as if it had never existed. Instead something unanimous was growing, something great and unusual. Perhaps heroic even? Or simply inevitable? Steadfastly growing, one could physically sense it filling everything in its path, seeping into the brain, the veins, making the muscles more resilient. And it was impossible to distinguish where it ended inside you, and where it began in your neighbour – in Krycheyev, Druzhynin, Popelnachenko. It was something universal and each person in it was a tiny, but necessary part. And this was understandable: storm clouds were appearing in black billows.

At present one could only hear the distant roar of the thunder, but the silence was growing thicker all around, and it could be rended by a fiery arrow at any moment. Who knew what was happening at this moment out there where the villages clustered together in small flocks amid the golden fields and the green woods? Was Harasymenko still alive, and the many others like him scattered far from town, dispersed in the chaos of rebellion and ruin? Where are you, how are you, our distant rural comrades…?

The silence in the room grew thicker still, and the candles flickered more mysteriously. Meanwhile Zivert's voice continued – businesslike, deliberate and calculated – without ranting or expressing a single note of pathos:

"…But first we must extract banditism's sting, tear out its tongue. We must finger well all these Prosvita members, these former members of the Ukrainian National Alliance… We must finally drag into the light of day these manufacturers of the insurgent ideology…!"

After these words something throbbed once again inside Horobenko and began to thump in his bosom, but he immediately quashed it. He even craned forward a little and once more listened greedily to Zivert. The man's tempered words attracted him, forced him to listen. He grabbed at the words while they were still fresh, before they had taken hackneyed root in his memory, like various other words from countless other speeches. Horobenko importunately strove to grasp who this man was. No, he wasn't wondering whether the fellow was a Latvian, a Pole or a Jew. No, it was not that at all. It was this. Where had he come from? Where had this dynamic figure appeared from, with these burning eyes and tempered words, as brilliant as the blade of a dagger? From the catacombs? From a Roman tavern where gladiators gathered to deliberate, or from an Inquisition tribunal, or the fires of the Taborites,[26] or maybe even from the underground People's Will[27]…?

That was not it at all. What comparisons could there be! It was realistic and simple: Zivert was the quintessential embodiment of this whole room, in general, of the thousands of such rooms lit by electricity or candles, with night-lamps and without, those rooms which had suddenly sprouted fresh buds on the dried wood of old life. This was the nerve, which had reacted most strongly when the instinct of Party self-preservation was aroused.

Horobenko looked intently into the lively, large sharp eyes, while his thoughts continued to paint a picture of Zivert.

…Zivert is one of the few who have already completely crossed yesterday's boundaries. Both I, and Chernyshov, and Drobot – we all are still only trudging along our paths, while he is already far on the other side. For this reason, Zivert (without posing, but quite naturally) has in him the poet, the accountant, the gentle lyre (yes, yes – who have I heard that from? – Zivert plays the violin beautifully, he's a virtuoso) and the bloodied sword. And so, it finally makes sense why the temperament of a savage and higher mathematics are so indivisibly entwined in Zivert.

These were people who, despite their past, had a determined habit of bringing matters to a conclusion. They had to conclude them or die. Actually, not die. That was the thing, they would never die. No matter what happened, they would continue to live in people's imaginations as a

---

26   A Christian faction within the Hussite movement in the medieval Lands of the Bohemian Crown, today's Czech Republic.

27   *Narodnaya Volya* was a 19th century revolutionary political organization in the Russian Empire, which advocated an indigenous socialism based upon the massive Russian peasantry.

legend, as brave, iron conquistadors who dared to be the first to step onto the unknown shores of social truth.

In their footsteps, drenched in their blood and the blood of other people, there would grow the chrysanthemums of poems, novels and folk tales.

In the memoirs of future generations these small Ziverts would join the ranks of Marat, Robespierre, Dombrovsky, Delescluze, Gonta and Zalizniak.[28] Herein lay the strength and beauty of Zivert, and with him this whole confusion, all these disturbing days, mobilized to the very last minute…!

With his small hand Zivert brought a glass of water to his mouth and took several energetic gulps. Then his face tensed once more, the wrinkles drifted back to his eyes and seemed to take aim, ready to pounce.

"…The bandit must be squashed, otherwise he will squash us! We must send our best comrades to the villages without delay. The whole Party organism must be flexed and each of its members must be severely accounted for."

Zivert's sharp gestures were redolent of an enormous charge of energy and importunate obstinacy. It was somehow strange to watch his small, insignificant figure and it became simply incomprehensible how such strong sense of will and indefatigable energy could fit into him. And it seemed as if this figure had appeared here quite by accident, seeming to become attached to Zivert's eyes through some misunderstanding, and one felt sorry for this weedy body which was incapable of absorbing all of Zivert's energy, and for the oversized field jacket which dangled about like a scarecrow's clothes in a strong wind…

---

28   Names of people who had headed uprisings and rebellions.

Like two miniature headlamps, the lenses of a pince-nez flashed at the front table, and Krycheyev rose slowly to his feet.

Horobenko stopped breathing and became all ears. Each surname read out fell in an echoing drop and disappeared.

…Zavadsky, Khomenko, Chernyshov, Kitsys, Druzhynin…

"I understand, Chernyshov and Druzhynin are on the list, but where's my name…?"

The drops continued to fall. Measured, distinct, resonant:

…Frolov, Potriasov, Khudoliy…

And once more Horobenko recalled Zivert's words: 'we must send our best comrades'.

Horobenko asked himself once more:

"The best ones? Well, yes – Druzhynin, Khomenko, who else is there?"

Krycheyev's lenses glinted once more:

"All these comrades are to come to the Party Committee office tomorrow to receive their mandates and weapons. The meeting is closed…"

Horobenko could still not accept that the list had been fully read out. The flames of candles danced all about him.

Only after the whole room, right up to the ceiling and out through the open windows into the street, became filled with the sounds of *The International*, the singing reflecting a stubborn will to struggle and overcome, did Horobenko realize that the list of those who had been mobilized had been exhausted and did not include himself…

He didn't feel like returning home. A full moon, etched at the edges, placidly continued to rise above the square to its eternal aimless goal, and this aimlessness and eternity made the soul feel easier and calmer.

The silvery-green stream which came in at an angle from above, deathly and continuous, inundated the square, the provincial houses and the lindens, making the town look a little fanciful, mournful, nicer. Kost walked past the spreading lindens surrounding the church cemetery and continued blindly down Staro-Kyivska Street.

The hour was late. The street stretched out before him deserted, quite dead, and only somewhere in the distance where the moonlight had woven an exacting, magical crypt out of the trees, was someone's dog barking lazily, hollowly.

Martial law was in place and the plebs – some fearfully, others obediently – were long since asleep. And that was very good.

Kost would not get in their way, and they would stay out of his.

Sleep your peaceful sweet sleep, plebs! You probably don't even imagine what an essentially good thing peaceful, carefree sleep is…! However, Kost Horobenko would not fall asleep on this night. There was no need for sleep. The houses could nap, and the dog could bark out of boredom. Kost wanted peace. The moon would continue its silver, silent downpour, while the familiar, taciturn, empty street would tell Kost so much. Kost would gladly listen to its rather simple, provincial account. This might appear funny viewed from afar, but in the end each person was free to do whatever gave him pleasure and joy.

Kost walked along quietly along the edge of the footpath, deep in thought, and behind him the moon struggled to slip out of the trees, to continue rolling on toward unknown heavenly maelstroms – without any cares or worries.

XIX

Kost Horobenko did not know himself why he had come to the art workshop today. Certainly not because today the workshop would be having live 'models' for the first time and these models would be naked White Guard women. What did Kost care about them? Wasn't it all the same how this White labour was being utilized? Whether these women were washing floors in offices, or peeling potatoes, or posing? Indeed, it made no difference at all to Kost. And besides, this was a matter decided by the Judicial Section, the political bureau or whoever else. It was all the same to Kost – he had simply come to check on the work of the workshop.

After all, since its opening, since the meeting at the opening, he had not been back here.

The students had already arrived. For the most part they were Red Army soldiers from the local guards company, several young Komsomol faces, and two elderly workers. They sat down on the low, uncomfortable school desks, which had been brought here from some school and began sharpening their pencils, bringing out their erasers. The youngish pug-nosed workshop commandant, Kolka Nosov, handed out paper to the students, as if they were pupils, and the workshop prepared to begin work.

Awkward in his movements, unshaven, flabby in appearance, Fitskhelaurov, the workshop instructor, deemed it necessary to warn his auditorium:

"Today, *tovarishchi*, we will be sketching two women. I would ask you to work quietly…" He had wanted to say: 'without cracking jokes', but looking across at Horobenko, he changed his mind and corrected himself: "So I would ask you not to disturb the comrade women posing for us. Now please get ready… Comrade Nosov, please…" he addressed the commandant.

This warning and a certain note of solemnity in Fitskhelaurov's words did not please Horobenko. He should be doing it simply, without this preamble!

Fitskhelaurov walked in front of the desks with a heavy elephant's gait and threw a sideways glance at Horobenko once more. It was no ordinary look: at first wrinkles gathered around the corners of his eyes (obviously the small muscles were working actively under his skin), and then the eyelids rose automatically, revealing two sparkling dark eyes. Horobenko hated this look even more. He thought: 'He seems a very uncertain type… Where did he appear from in this town?'

Behind the door in the adjoining room the workshop commandant Kolka Nosov was fussing about, explaining something to someone. He had fashioned a curtain at the side near the door and when they heard the rustle of a woman's dress behind the curtain, the faint crackle of clasps and hooks, the auditorium pricked up its ears and became more serious. Everyone's face seemed to grow narrower and became a shade paler.

And then a woman in a grey bathing robe quietly stepped out onto the dais from behind the curtain. Pale-faced, without raising her eyes from the floor, she took several steps and stopped. The large clumsy robe covered her as if she was a hospital patient. The woman was nervous.

Fitskhelaurov hurried up to her and politely offered her a stool.

"If you please. Will you allow me to take it off?" Without waiting for a reply Fitskhelaurov touched the shoulders of the robe and it fell to the floor, baring the whiteness of breasts, hips and legs. The woman flinched and involuntarily, bashfully covered the pink buds of her breasts with her hands. She looked at the auditorium apprehensively and her cheeks flushed red.

Though far too courteous, Fitskhelaurov was meanwhile adroitly pottering around her.

"Your surname, if you please?"

The auditorium had become rooted to their desks and stopped breathing.

The woman blushed even more and whispered barely audibly:

"Shigorina…"

"Please, *tovarishch* Shigorina… If you please – move your head a little to the left and back… no, no – only a little bit. Please, allow me to correct you."

Like a surgeon, Fitskhelaurov stiffly grabbed the woman's temples and twisted them around. The woman turned her head obediently.

"Thrust your breast out more… Like this. Great. Hold this pose, if you don't mind."

Fitskhelaurov intently studied the woman's pose once more and then turned to face the desks:

"We will begin, *tovarishchi*! Please…"

The students began to draw indecisively, their hands uncertainly roughing in the outlines of her pretty shoulders and hair. Meanwhile the woman had calmed down somewhat and was slowly becoming accustomed to her pose. Her black unplaited hair was tied at the back with a ribbon and fell heavily behind her back, but one lock had strayed and rested on her breasts. This obviously appealed to the woman. She sneaked a look at it, as if checking the effect this would have on the onlookers, and then ran a curious, experienced eye over the students.

Fitskhelaurov came up to her once more.

"How long can you hold this pose?"

The woman became embarrassed and replied hastily:

"No, no, please… I'll ask to rest when I'm tired."

Fitskhelaurov shuffled off among the desks to correct the students' work. Horobenko sat down on a chair against the wall under a poster. The woman rested her curious black eyes on him and Horobenko imagined that she shrugged her shoulder, flirting with him.

Their gazes suddenly fused together, and the woman felt as if she had been scalded: unable to stand it, she transferred her gaze to the dais.

Now Horobenko knew why he had come here. Yes, he needed to come here. He needed to look into these black eyes, into their very vacant depths to despise them. Yes – despise them! As an intellectual, Kostyk, you lacked contempt, that sacred contempt, without which there can be no great love. But now you will have it. You will! This woman before you is the petal of a reactionary lily. Do you remember her? She too is a small, but vivid fragment from your past. Remember? The hussar regiment in this very same town, parades, grand officers, New Year's Eve and Easter balls, and a masquerade party on Epiphany. You never saw that. You only knew about it. Heard about it. And then there was the district cinema, where every three days they showed new films.

Which were either 'eminent, dramatical, or comical.'

The only difference being that they were either 'supremely eminent' or 'painfully dramatical', or 'powerfully comical'. And so it went every three days. Repeated again and again. Remember, Kostyk? Those were your high school years. You didn't yet know Nadia then.

There you were, a small, shy high school student, staring at the third row from a corner of the foyer near the door, eyeing the black astrakhan fur and the broad brimmed hat under the ostrich feathers. You could only look at the hat, for those black eyes never looked back at you. Spurs tinkled around the hat, hussar shoulder-straps flashed, and the gaze and smile of the black eyes was only for them.

And one day, in this very cinema, as people were leaving the séance, the lady in the astrakhan fur coat dropped her compact. You rushed to the ground, grabbed the compact with trembling, childish hands and handed it to her. Only then, for a moment, did the black eyes look at you and smile sweetly, as if tossing you a tip. That was the only time…

And now these eyes had looked at you a second time. But you can clearly see for yourself that she was no unattainable queen from enchanting dreams, as it had seemed to you then at the cinema. She was now an officer's wife. The owner of precious wares – a beautiful body and black eyes. She had nothing else apart from this. After someone nationalized these last assets of hers, she would become a very repugnant beggar. An ordinary streetwalker. Indeed, Mysha Chernyshov was right not to worry about their feelings as nude models. And this nice wild pussycat knew only too well the listed price of her wares on life's stock-exchange in our domestic Soviet conditions. Yes, yes. There you have it.

The woman really was quite herself now and posed without the slightest bit of shame or embarrassment. Occasionally she would involuntarily adjust the sumptuous black hair on her temples and then her straight, refined hands rose lightly, her pretty elbow bulged, and the dark patches under her arms became barely noticeable.

This had an effect on the auditorium. People began to wheeze softly, whisper stealthily, but in any case, everyone was now drawing briskly and assiduously. Some of the fellows even let drop witticisms.

With feigned weariness the woman would languidly throw her head back, then her breasts jiggled slightly, and after this, with a barely noticeable smile, her eyes wandered triumphantly about the studio until they came across Horobenko or Fitskhelaurov. Then she pretended once more to become embarrassed and ashamed. Horobenko looked with disgust at her face and thought:

'Another three sittings and she'll feel quite at home here. She'll begin to flirt with someone or even start an affair with Fitskhelaurov. If not in reality, then at least in her imagination, for she's essentially a proper whore.'

Horobenko smiled viciously:

"And this is that 'blue blood' people speak of…!'

Fitskhelaurov helped the woman on with her robe.

"Thank you. That's enough for the first time… You must be tired… Please."

He offered her his hand as she left the dais and the woman gracefully disappeared behind the curtain.

Commandant Kolka Nosov called out from the door:

"Ahlaya Kanonova! Your turn. Come out."

Once more a dress rustled behind the curtain, snap fasteners hastily crackled and far sooner than the auditorium had expected, a second woman emerged from behind the curtain. She took a step toward the dais but suddenly, with a sweeping gesture, as if remembering, shed her robe like a black pair of wings and stepped haughtily naked onto the dais.

This woman was neither embarrassed nor ashamed. She threw her head back and insolently, defiantly stared ahead, somewhere beyond the wall, over the heads of the students. Her chestnut hair spilled over her tender back in waves and light from the window gave it a silvery lustre. Her long lashes slightly concealed her large, azure eyes, but their dusky moistness burned with so much anger, hatred and contempt, that even Fitskhelaurov became a little disconcerted. He was standing between her and the desks, nervously rubbing his puffy hands together, which seemed to be made of dough. The students opened their mouths like simpletons and stared in astonishment at the model.

The woman shook her head a little and her small lips, looking as if they had been engraved, twitched at the corners in displeasure.

"I'm ready! What do I do?" she said in Russian.

This brought Fitskhelaurov back to life and gave him back his usual poise. He moved agilely about the dais, setting up the stool, transferring his papers from the dais to the windowsill for some reason, as if they might have hidden the woman from the view of the students, and set about positioning her.

Horobenko no longer heard his relentless, professional phrases. This slender woman had almost blinded everyone with her truly exceptional bared beauty. It was hard to look at her beautiful naked figure, and at the same time one was terribly attracted to stare at it. There was something strong about this beauty. Strong and cruel.

Fitskhelaurov stretched his hands out to the model's face:

"A little to the left… allow me to correct you…"

The woman stopped him with a slight movement of her hand.

"No. I'll do it myself…"

The woman said this simply, but so firmly that Fitskhelaurov's hands immediately fell to his sides, as if someone had unexpectedly struck them with a riding-crop.

Fitskhelaurov stepped down from the dais and ingratiatingly announced in a lowered, muffled voice:

"When you become tired, be kind enough to let me know…"

"Thank you."

As if tied down, the woman froze to the stool in the required pose. Her hands held the edge of the stool firmly; her springy, almost girlish breasts were thrust at the students, and her eyes rested somewhere on the cornices above. The woman remained quite placid, she even seemed to be conscientiously carrying out Fitskhelaurov's instructions. Yet in her whole pose, in that gaze thrown far above the people surrounding her, there was so much independence and disdain, that it seemed this was no imprisoned officer's wife sitting here, but some queen from the gloom of the Middle Ages who would presently be giving orders to her aides and servants.

And that was the way it was. Chained to her pose on the stool, this woman had captivated the auditorium the moment she appeared. She had grabbed everyone present with her thin marble fingers and the small pearl-shell nails on their tips and pressed them painfully against the stool. None of the students were drawing. Only the two elderly workers set about sluggishly roughing in her forehead, but nothing decent came of it. A patch of light rested on her forehead, but it seemed as if it was a burning star and the woman was not at all naked, but dressed in a thin, priceless tunic. No one noticed her nakedness.

The students looked devoutly at her face, and their eyes misted over, filled with sorrow, becoming veiled with a desperate grief. Many of them had seen pretty and ugly women. They had caressed them, kissed them and made love to them. Those women had become lost in the eternal torrent of days, become erased like an old ink-spot. However, none of them had seen a woman like this before. From the very bottom of their souls, crumpled in the echelons of the

revolution, this woman was revealing forgotten fairy tales told by long-dead grannies about princesses, faraway kingdoms and the firebird…

This woman was indeed out of a fairy tale. She was sitting completely naked before them, but never would this fascinating body ever belong to any of them, not even a smile or a gentle glance could be wrestled from her tightly-pursed lips and open white forehead, poised to resist.

This woman could be undressed, but not bent, not thrown to the ground – never.

She had come to them from a fairy tale, from non-existence, and would return there.

Her beauty, the quintessence of all the past shattered years, did not belong to them. This body had given its insane caresses to someone they had crushed with laughter and indifference. What mighty vanquisher would appear to tame this woman? Who would come up and place this priceless diamond in his pocket as if it was his own? It lay here now, exasperating the hungry crowd!

It was melancholy to sit here and watch this haughty, untamed beauty. Wrong and painful…

Fitskhelaurov did not dare upset the tumescent silence. He walked quietly on tip-toe in front of the desks and did not bother with the students. Only when he turned around did he steal a glance at the model, like some pickpocket, and thought: 'She would be just right for painting Boyarina Morozova.[29] Exquisite! An exceptionally rare specimen…!'

---

29   Famous painting by V. Surikov done in 1887 depicting a defiant

Horobenko felt bad. From his position he could clearly see her full face and her hard, slightly moist eyes. Even when she had stepped onto the dais, he had thought: she looks like she's climbing a scaffold. The best final clots of corrupt aristocratic blood had probably gone to the guillotine like that during the French Revolution. She was an inveterate enemy. If her side were to return tomorrow, that tender arm with its transparent azure veins would imperiously show these students the way to the gallows; these gentle fingers would grip a parasol and pick out the eyes of prisoners with it. And these large deep eyes would most certainly laugh then. Oh, they would no doubt laugh! But that was only if...!

Horobenko looked malevolently at the naked model, but at the same time he felt troubled, something gnawed at him, something disturbed him.

He looked at the student sitting at one end whose pencil was poised thoughtlessly above the paper, his eyes immersed in the model, and turned away.

This farce with the nude model had to be stopped and Fitskhelaurov needed to be removed first of all. He was quite unsuited.

But Horobenko could find no way to break this numbing spell. He felt very small, short, and not at all in control.

The woman became tired of sitting in the same pose and stirred. Horobenko sensed the auditorium come alive and then freeze once more. Fitskhelaurov stopped near the desks and tugged at the hairs on his chin.

And suddenly a desk lid crashed loudly.

The woman continued sitting placidly in the same pose.

Heavy footsteps thumped loudly across the floor, accompanied by the creak of swollen soldier's boots. A

---

noblewoman who refused a life of luxury and embarked on a struggle with the tsarist government and the official church.

thin, slightly emotional Red Army soldier was making his way toward Horobenko. Slowly, procrastinating, he dragged his feet one ahead of the other, as if wanting to extend the time before he reached Horobenko. At last he reached him, his eyes darted about guiltily, he scratched the back of his neck and said:

"Comrade administrator…" the Red Army soldier leaned his dishevelled head down to Horobenko's ear and said in a low voice:

"You can't draw like this… Look," and he pointed with his head, "see, people are out of their minds… *Da*, we too are, that is… All men breathe harder…"

Horobenko gave the Red Army soldier a hostile look and said curtly:

"What's the matter? What is it you want to say…?"

The Red Army soldier scratched the back of his neck once more:

"If you could maybe send us some others… It's simply that…"

It was as if someone had punched Horobenko. He bit his lip, rose to his feet and almost yelled out:

"That's none of your business…! If you don't like it, don't attend! No one's forcing you to come here…"

The Red Army soldier straightened and bashfully shuffled from foot to foot. "*Da*, I only mentioned it… Don't get me wrong…"

Fitskhelaurov was hurrying toward them to see what had transpired.

BORYS ANTONENKO-DAVYDOVYCH

XX

Up ahead the two coffins swayed steadily and silently. They swung a little to the left, then moved across to the other side. Then to the left once more and back again.

Like leaders exhausted in battle, the black and red flags moved quietly behind the coffins. The two deceased seemed to float along more easily under their canopy on this final journey.

There was a long row of wreaths up ahead. Simple, insignificant wreaths out of fir branches and field flowers, bound together with red ribbons. These ribbons fell sorrowfully toward the ground, seeming to leave a red path behind them.

And right behind the coffins rose the shrill lament of Frolova, wrapped in a black scarf, and the quiet, almost fearful sobs of the hunched figure of Chernyshov's astonishingly tiny old mother.

The Party members followed the coffins mournfully and in silence. They moved not in rows, but in an entangled, huddled crowd.

And there were no words on their lips, no songs, there was no monotonous whine or the funereal knell of a church bell.

Feet stepped heavily and silently through the dust and only the orchestra grieved behind the flags with the sorrowful chords of some doleful march. Those chords were a blend of the thoughts, words and singing of individual Party members. They combined and carried their murky, melancholy waters somewhere far, far away beyond the azure horizons of existence… It was strange to see oneself in this crowd among the alien and indifferent old-fashioned provincial houses and meanwhile the insolently curious looks of the plebs were insufferable.

Horobenko did not notice this straight away. The scene entered his eyes at first, stumbled about in his brain, and only then did it settle there in a sticky, insipid vapour. And then he noticed the plebs standing by their gates and gawking at the procession.

They were not averse to hearing a brass band, and they wanted to have a good look at the way communists buried their dead.

There were many of them and the crowd of Party members among them were like a handful of Columbus' sailors on the American continent among throngs of savages.

And he also noticed:

Some of them stayed with the procession and ran ahead with a skip, to have a look at the communist mother and wife. They were amazed by the small, shrivelled form of Chernyshov's mother. She probably even disappointed them, for she was an ordinary old mother, like millions of other mothers who quietly and submissively fretted over their children.

They were not satisfied, and now two of them moved quite close to the coffins and stood on tiptoe to take look at the faces of the dead men.

Horobenko saw this as an insult to the deceased. Someone should bawl these curious people out, make them dash off to their mouseholes.

Up ahead in those two coffins lay the first victims of the latest skirmish between the Party and these people. Mysha Chernyshov and Frolov… These were those best ones, as Zivert had said, whom the Party had sent into the countryside. Their bodies were covered with red nankeen and luckily the plebs could not see their faces. But Horobenko knew – he had seen the bloodstained corpses on the carts after they had been brought to the Military Commissariat – Chernyshov's right ear had been ripped off and he had a bluish-burgundy stripe across his forehead; Frolov had a gory hole in one eye and horror stared out of the other. That eye had seen only enemies in its last living moments. Inveterate, savage, furious enemies. It was unpleasant to look at those faces, but at the same time they drew one's gaze toward them.

But their terrible suffering had passed, and the corpses now lay placidly in the coffins, as if resting after an exhausting day at work. Horobenko wanted it to be him lying there, not Chernyshov, and let the trumpets weep just the same then and the flags whisper quietly among themselves... And let there be no outsiders, no strangers. Not even these Red Army soldiers from the guards company marching behind them.

Let only our own people turn up for this secret, majestic council of life and death, only those who had been soldered with hot young blood into a living steel chain...

*   *   *

As the procession drew up to the cemetery gates the half-blind old caretaker hurried off to the belltower out of habit to welcome the dead with bells. A bell rang hollowly, sepulchrally in the low wooden belltower and its sounds became lost in the pine trees. Then a second thin one, a third one – thinner still, a fourth sounding a treble note, and again that hollow, drawn-out octave... Bom... bam... bim... di-i-in... bo-o-om...

True chimes of death.

Someone broke away from the crowd and dashed headlong to stop the bell-ringer. To immediately put an end to this mockery over the bodies of their comrades!

And then the trumpets wailed again.

It was unusual and strange for the old cemetery to suddenly host this large crowd of communists with their flags. And the old crosses with their peeling paint seemed to cower, ready to hobble off into dark corners. The young slender pines froze in amazement, as if preparing to listen to the speeches.

The familiar old cemetery.

With the same old paths among the graves, only now they were overgrown with green grass and the odd immortelle.

Immortelles in the cemetery! This was an interesting coincidence: a cellar of bones and rotting flesh, and above it – immortal flowers…!

But the revolution had disturbed the cemetery too. On an unbridled mustang it had flown over the immortelles and now overturned crosses lay on the ground, gravestones had been smashed, and photographs of the deceased had been ripped out of their oval frames.

Ruins. Dust.

And this was good. All cemeteries should be razed to the ground, so that not one of them would remind people of the past! For the cemetery was not only here. Was not that county town, which spread out lazily beyond here, a cemetery as well? Every corner there had absorbed the past and it stuck out in full view – as a witness or a silent reproach… And this gravestone lying near the road, it too was from there, from that past which had been buried in the town. This gravestone had an inscription – Kost remembered it:

The soul will never forget –
You hath but only one,
Only one mother.
Never, never.

Horobenko came up to the gravestone deliberately.

Yes, the words were still there, only they had grown black and become covered with dust. The pine tree thrust its top into the distant sky the same way, and the azure sky peered through its branches with tender eyes, seeming to smile tearfully. And the figure of the inspired girl forever whispering a prayer beside the gravestone was now sullied, her white marble lips assiduously painted red.

Colour in these relics of human hypocrisy and lies, you young insolent unknown hands! Smash these worthless old crosses and trample these graves! There's no need for cemeteries. Let there be only the green serenity of the pines. And nothing else…

The holes had been dug some distance from the other graves, where the young pines still grew wild, where the grave diggers had hitherto left the ground untouched. As the procession drew closer and the fresh holes became visible, everyone stirred strangely. A barely audible rustle passed through the crowd and the people bunched together, but that was only for a moment. Slowly everyone surrounded the holes in a thick living ring…

Krycheyev was the first to speak. He spoke loudly, without faltering, but there was something dry and official about his words, as if he was reading a proclamation. And the coffins stood here beside the holes, covered in red nankeen. Now one could sense more clearly that the coffins contained Mysha Chernyshov and Frolov. And it seemed incredible that Chernyshov was no more, that he wouldn't smile any more, utter that 'crawling rotters' of his,

his eyes would no longer burn with that childish twinkle. In the coffin there under the nankeen there now lay a disfigured strange face. These two corpses were frightening and yet at the same time much too dear. These were not the corpses of Frolov with his bourgeois habits and the flippant soak Mysha Chernyshov, no – they were the sacrifices for a single common cause. Maybe the flesh had not held out and there had been dying entreaties, recantations and groans, but maybe this had never happened… Death had expunged their faults, and the organization was burying two dear, cherished comrades. For this reason, shoulders pressed closer together and the crowd of communists looked at the bodies with a united grieving eye.

Zivert pushed his way through the thick of the crowd.

The pines pricked up their ears even more when his clear, chesty voice rang out:

"We were much too soft, comrades, much too humane. Now we must pay dearly for our softness. Our comrades are here. Until recently we saw them among us; they are the first whom we sent to our outposts. Look what has been done to them…! Just take a look…!"

Zivert stretched out his hand and bent over the coffins. A moment longer and it seemed Zivert would tear off the fabric to reveal the horrible darkened faces. One wanted to stop Zivert's hand: there's no need…!

However, Zivert straightened again and proclaimed to the crowd:

"The struggle is not over yet! The fight continues. For one of ours – ten of theirs, death for death!"

And Horobenko involuntarily repeated to himself:

"Death for death."

He repeated the words and became pensive.

The last to step toward the coffins was Druzhynin. He wanted to say a few words about his fallen comrades, to say that they had performed their duty, that thousands of Communards would suffer their fate, but the words became ponderous and he could not summon them, his throat was unable to voice them. Druzhynin was crumpling his soiled cap with his fingers and quite different words left his lips:

"Comrades…! Dear brothers… Farewell, comrades…"

Suddenly old Mrs. Chernyshov began to sob quietly on one side:

"Mysha… My Myshenka… My dear, beloved son…"

Druzhynin pressed his cap to his chest, swept the air with his other hand and disappeared in the crowd.

But there were no tears. They sprang forth somewhere inside him, from his heart.

The coffins were raised and slowly lowered into the holes. Then Mrs. Frolov let out a delirious scream and scrambled after the coffin. A salute exploded over their heads. Once, and a second time… And when the first spadeful of earth fell onto the coffins, the trumpets waved aside the old cemetery church, the crosses and pines and, boldly and triumphantly struck up the notes of *The International*. And these sailed across the fields to the distant taciturn villages, as if after a victory, like a hymn of eternal, immortal life…

And for a second time Horobenko remembered something, which had occurred to him before:

'Death cannot intersect the eternal kaleidoscope of life…!'

He only had to find that Archimedean lever within him, that pivot within himself, and hold it firmly in his hands. Then there would be a different, beautiful life and simple, logical death. As simple as with the Japanese soldier who, with a smile, salutes his own death before a firing squad. But there must be blood for blood, and death for death! And this was not said by Zivert here, they are my words.

Fresh clods of earth thudded loudly into the holes and all around the cemetery the pines rose toward the sky on their slender trunks. So green and young.

XXI

From the looks of the plebs – foreign, non-Party, smirk-
ing – from the whispers into neighbour's ears and from
the way in which the market hastily dispersed and emptied, and lastly from the way in which District Supply
Commissar Drobot raced past on horseback to the Party
Committee office – all this made Horobenko realize that
something had happened.

He emerged from the Cultural Section of the trade
union office and prepared to make his way to the Communist Dining Hall, however the air was uneasy, scorched
by the midday sun of July.

Something sweaty was lurking in it and breathing
heavily – something hostile, spiteful and passionate.
Horobenko turned left and went to the Party Committee
office. He hurried across the overgrown square near the
cathedral with its dry saplings standing forlornly in the
future Socialist Park and the unfinished pedestal of the
memorial to the victims of the first October battles, when
Radchenko came running up to him.

"You off to the Party Committee? A state of readiness
has been declared…"

Radchenko unbuttoned his shirt down to his hairy
chest, sweat dribbled from his shaven head, he wiped
himself with his sleeve and tried to catch his breath.

Horobenko stopped to let Radchenko rest and asked:
"What's actually happened?"

Radchenko looked at him in surprise:

"You don't know yet?"

"I've heard nothing."

"There's a gang in Koziyivka. Six miles from town… They killed three people on the road, as well as Harasymenko from Fedorivka… His chopped-off head was found in the forest…"

The Party Committee yard was crowded. There were a lot of armed people and Nestorenko's figure, laced up with straps, flashed past and disappeared into a door. Drobot was giving someone orders. Slavina moved uneasily from group to group and wordlessly listened in on conversations. Druzhynin was sitting on the stairs and wearily smoked a 'goat's paw' cigarette. Fresh Party members arrived off the street.

There was no need to ask questions. From snatches of conversation, from separate words, from everyone's utter seriousness, from the absence of any laughter, everything became immediately clear to Horobenko.

The town organization was passing into a state of readiness. All Party members were mobilized. The gang might be bold enough to attack the town. But the initiative must be wrested from it. The guards company and some of the Party members were assembling a detachment, which was to take Koziyivka that night. The rest of the people would be defending the town.

Horobenko ascended the stairs to Krycheyev's office on the second floor.

Krycheyev was deliberating about something with the organization instructor and Nestorenko. He was listening attentively.

Horobenko came up to Krycheyev.

"I'd like a few words with you, Comrade Krycheyev."

Krycheyev tore himself away from the conversation with displeasure and turned the lenses of his pince-nez toward Horobenko.

"What's wrong?"

"I'd like to speak in private…"

Popelnachenko looked in astonishment at Horobenko.

Two deep wrinkles drew together on Krycheyev's forehead. He rose from the table and apprehensively accompanied Horobenko to the window.

"What's wrong? I'm listening…"

Horobenko looked intently through Krycheyev's pince-nez into his eyes, paused for a moment, and then said firmly:

"I've come to ask you, actually, not ask, but demand that you send me with the detachment to Koziyivka…"

Krycheyev raised his eyebrows, then screwed up his eyes suspiciously:

"Why are you – I don't understand – asking such a thing of me? We need people here too. The town is in danger."

Horobenko repeated obstinately:

"Send me to Koziyivka. It has to be this way…! For me. D'you understand?"

Krycheyev rubbed his cheek and, as if spying something new and hitherto unknown in Horobenko, looked him intently in the eye.

"Of course, I have nothing against it. If that's what you want – please, I'll tell Nestorenko to add your name to the list."

Horobenko announced forcefully:

"Yes, that's what I want!"

Krycheyev returned to his desk, while Horobenko made his way to the door. He heard everyone move from their places behind him and whisper to Krycheyev. Popelnachenko's sharp, questioning gaze pressed against his back. He wanted to turn around to face the eyes but decided against it and stepped outside.

Slavina was pestering Druzhynin. She was telling him in a whisper:

"I don't understand, why include women in the state of readiness? We won't really be shooting at bandits, will we!"

Druzhynin answered reluctantly, in Russian:

"It's better for you this way. Indeed, if we all stay together, it will be somehow more loyal, yes, and in general…"

Zavalny drove into the yard with two carts. He had brought beef and tobacco for the Party members.

All laced-up, Nestorenko slid out the door. On his head he wore a chunky Kuban hat, a Cossack sabre hung at his left side, and on his right side was a sawn-off rifle. He was all attention and seemed to have grown taller. His face was stern, his voice sharp and commanding.

"Those who haven't yet received rifles – you can get them from the organization instructor."

Slavina asked timidly:

"The women too?"

Without looking at her, Nestorenko answered angrily:

"*Da, da*! You heard me – everyone."

Nestorenko swung around on his heel in military fashion and disappeared in the doorway.

Holtsev was handing out the rifles. After the incident with the Party committee reference to the *guberniya*, Horobenko had somehow failed to notice Holtsev. He seemed to have disappeared from town. Holtsev assiduously counted out the cartridges, carefully took a rifle from the corner, spent a minute examining it from the stock to the front sights, as if admiring it, and only then handed it over to the Party member.

"Please. It's not loaded."

As soon as Horobenko entered, Holtsev noticed him at once, as if he had specially been waiting for him. He joyously took off his cap for some reason, hastily threw on his mask of a smile, and greeted Horobenko like an old friend.

"A-ah! Comrade Horobenko! Please, please…"

Horobenko sedately returned the greeting.

Holtsev selected a smart cavalry rifle and handed it to Horobenko.

"This one will be fine for you. It's light. What about a cartridge pouch, have you got one…? Wait. I'll find one. I've put one aside here for you."

Holtsev moved up a chair and stood on it to rummage about under the papers on the cupboard, while Horobenko wondered once more:

'Why is he so sickly sweet toward me…?'

Holtsev deftly filled the pouch with cartridge clips, tied the straps and handed it over to Horobenko:

"That's all now. Here you are."

He squinted with one eye and asked in a whisper:

"Where you going – to Koziyivka or staying here?"

Horobenko said stiffly:

"I don't know."

Holtsev leaned over to Horobenko's ear and, spraying spittle, whispered:

"I'll have a word with Popynaka to have you posted here…"

Horobenko flinched, looked Holtsev sharply in the eye (Holtsev threw a mask over his face once more) and bluntly hammered out every word:

"I in no way authorize you to act on my behalf, and in general, please leave me in peace!"

Holtsev smiled guiltily and minced the air with his fingers.

"Come on, why act this way, by god! It wasn't at all because…"

Horobenko no longer heard him. He threw the rifle over his shoulder and was already on the steps leading outside.

Next to the brick woodshed he saw Drobot recounting some obscene anecdote to a group of Party members. He was smiling lewdly with his large thick lips. Someone was breaking into guffaws, while Nestorenko stood silently nearby and listened in attentive silence.

The street kids were up to their mischievous business behind the fence. They were sending someone up and ecstatically yelled out *The International*; suddenly a blond, shaggy head appeared over the fence, small cunning grey eyes darted about the yard, rested on Nestorenko, and a thin childish voice broke out in a wavering soprano:

> *In a meadow Trotsky sat,*
> *Champing on a horse's shank.*
> *'Oh yes, what nasty business*
> *This Soviet beef really is!'*

Nestorenko immediately turned toward the fence. The tousled head disappeared. Nestorenko spat and swore. Drobot became silent and looked at the fence. The same childish voice continued taunting them from behind the fence:

> *Eh, yeah, the apple's lightly marinated!*
> *But Soviet power is quite demented…*

Nestorenko called out angrily to someone:

"Catch that brat and rip 'is ears off!"

Druzhynin answered from the porch:

"Why such reactions, Comrade Nestorenko? Brats should be educated, not beaten."

Everyone became quiet behind the fence.

A machine-gun was brought into the yard and placed near the porch. As if not understanding who it actually had to spit on, the machine-gun spread out its legs awkwardly and stared ridiculously at the old weathercock on the woodshed. A group of Komsomol members burst into song near the gate.

The rye there in the fields
Trampled by horse's hooves...

The sorrowful, drawn-out motif suddenly broke off and began to skip with a merry refrain:

In the shade of a white birch tree
A young Cossack was slain...

Horobenko listened to the song. It was an unusual one for the Party committee yard. Someone seemed to have brought it here on purpose from the former Prosvita or the current village school.

Zavalny left the Party committee office, having finished dealing with the food. He heard the song from the porch and joined in with his deep voice, which sounded like an untuned piano:

...Slain, oh slain he was,
Dragged into the rye...

And once again the song rejoiced for some reason, smiling tactlessly:

A crimson cloth of soft nankeen
Now covers his fair face...

'Our songs are strange,' Horobenko thought and lit up a cigarette. 'They grieve and laugh at the same time. They are strange, just like our whole fanciful history, which began with Khmelnytsky's times and ended with 'mother-Ukraine' and Kotliarevsky's *Aeneid*,[30] only to reawaken in 1918, turning the pathos of its rebirth into an embroidered farce… How odd our history is…'

"Communards, fall in!" Nestorenko's orders rang out from the middle of the yard.

The Party members formed up in disorderly fashion, assembling, dividing into two rows. Horobenko adjusted the rifle sling on his shoulder and pleasurably sucked on a commissariat supplied cigarette.

Nestorenko ran a commander's eye over the rows, but on reaching Horobenko his eyes stopped and glinted malevolently.

"And what about you?"

Horobenko failed to understand: "What's the problem, comrade?"

Nestorenko took a step toward him and shouted sternly:

"Get rid of that cigarette! Once the order for 'eyes front' has been given, there are to be no cigarettes. You're standing in line…!" he remarked to Horobenko, angry and offended, and moved away.

Like an innocent boy who had been punished, Horobenko could find nothing to say in reply. Although he immediately threw away the cigarette, as if it had scalded him, and stood in line blushing up to his ears.

And only after Nestorenko began reading out the orders from the right flank did Horobenko's brain sputter:

---

30   The Ukrainian writer Ivan Kotliarevsky wrote a "Ukrainianized" version of *The Aeneid*, in which Cossacks replaced the Greek personages of Virgil's original.

'He's a tsarist sergeant-major! A real sergeant-major!'

And then his chest began to burn, and his lips wanted to utter:

'Why didn't I answer back! I should have straight away...'

Nestorenko continued reading there from the right flank:

"...Solovyov, Bukrabo, Panasiuk, Horobenko, Kolot – these comrades will leave with the guards company for Koziyivka. Two steps forward!"

Horobenko moved forward two paces together with the rest of the people and suddenly felt someone's intent gaze on himself. He looked to the left. Popelnachenko was standing on the porch, leaning against the doorpost.

XXII

They set off close to eleven at night. Up front was the detachment of Communards, behind them two carts with machine-guns, followed by the guards company.

The night was dark, and a wary silence held the district town in its black paws. The town was asleep, and not a leaf rustled on the trees, not a single wicket gate creaked. Only above their heads, in the dark-green Milky Way, stellar snowstorms erupted, rushing tempestuously through the heavenly spaces, then dying away, scattering as tiny golden snowflakes, now placidly twinkling on the broken Pleiades or the Dipper, suspended in the sky like a discarded saucepan.

It was strange seeing those snowstorms in the cold heavens when one was still surrounded by an August night.

They walked in silence along the town's familiar streets. Their steps resounded firmly, like those of disciplined soldiers. It was hard to distinguish individual people. They all looked the same now. Both Zavalny, who was marching right next to him, and Drobot in the front row on the right, and this woman to his left who was taking larger than normal strides so as to keep up with the men. Who was she…? Leontieva, head of the Women's Section. She had a holster at her side with a Browning, and a small Austrian carbine on her back. Her closely-cropped hair topped with a cap was bent forward a little: she was trying to make sure she was in step with her comrades.

And once more Horobenko found it incomprehensible: where had this militarism of theirs appeared from? Until recently Leontieva was a worker in a large tobacco factory. She should have found this militarism repugnant. And yet – here she was, purposefully straightening her back, thrusting her chest forward, as if this had been an innate part of her military bearing.

'I still don't know them very well...' Horobenko thought. 'Maybe there is some sense, in the end, to this militarism, Nestorenko's straps, or put simply, Nestorenko's sergeant-majorism... Perhaps it is only my intellectual prejudices, which stop me from accepting this as something ordinary, necessary and inevitable... Who knows, maybe...'

Nestorenko rode on a strong grey mare to one side of the detachment. He sat as if glued to the mare. The night had thrown its dark mantle over them, making Nestorenko and his mare appear like a giant black centaur.

Horobenko strained his eyes to examine their outlines better. He obtained a unique loathsome pleasure from observing Nestorenko's figure, imagining the details of his dark face, with its thin chapped lips and small greenish eyes under a protruding shock of hair. Only he could not understand at all how this tight knot of brute force could influence grown intelligent people so strongly, and lead them off obediently, as if on a tether, to somewhere where only brute force was needed? No matter what, Kost, but you too succumbed to this force, it broke you back there in the Party committee yard with that cigarette and will lead you wherever it wishes.

They passed the last houses on the outskirts. Here the district town shed its genteel attire and gradually tightened its peasant drawstring. On a nearby knoll stood a taciturn scowling windmill, its long arms spread out wide, as if hissing to someone in the rear to hide in the fields. The two carts with mounted machine-guns creaked over the potholes.

Nestorenko stopped his mare to await the guards company. Horobenko passed quite close to him. He even thought that he had seen Nestorenko's eyes – they were cold, like tin at night, but piercing, with a savage glint. He wanted to look deeper into Nestorenko's eyes, to fathom the source of his strength and to break free of it. Horobenko tried to convince himself:

'It's not at all that 'he's leading' us, because first and foremost I am going there of my own free will. Going to liquidate the gang. I am going together with Popelnachenko, Drobot and Leontieva to kill and even execute those last ignorant peasants who want to destroy us in the name of their grain bins and wildly fanciful 'Mother Ukraine'. This is something which I've in fact long since wanted, and Nestorenko is here only coincidentally.'

They moved along the road beside the stubble. A large reddish moon crawled out from behind the houses of a distant settlement. Its wrinkled, bloated disc resembled a rachitic infant and its flat wry face refused to shine. A quail was screaming somewhere in the stubble.

The Communard detachment was moving freely now, no longer staying in line. Only Nestorenko continued riding in the same position off to one side – black and morose. Dew settled in cold droplets on the rifle barrels, the trodden dust of the road squished softly underfoot.

Nestorenko stopped his mare again and turned around in the saddle. He looked over the detachment and ordered in a low, hoarse voice:

"No more smoking! Guards company commander Hvozdev! Despatch a lookout sentry, there could be an attack from the north-south…"

'Stupid fool!' Horobenko thought. 'He means from the north-west. Can't even differentiate directions. What a commander…!'

However, Horobenko stopped himself one final time and began to reproach himself again:

'This, Kost, is intellectualism too! Rotten and good-for-nothing intellectualism. In the final analysis, it isn't that, unlike you, he can't differentiate the points of the compass… But the fact is that… Yes, exactly what is it?' Horobenko asked himself impatiently.

In the distance a mist hung over the Vorskla River against the backdrop of a black wall of forest. The moon had composed itself, climbed higher and released its feeble rays. Foreheads became faintly silvered and rifle barrels gleamed from time to time.

'The fact of the matter is, Kost, that you are marching against the village. The Ukrainian village. That only certain national watershed in whose name you once established Prosvitas, acted as an instructor for the Central Rada and retreated with the Directory's armies. Together with these incomprehensible people, you must now strike the very target, which you only recently built with your very own hands as a secure shield. You must shatter this target to pieces, so that no trace of it remains. You must shoot at your former self, Kost! That is the point…'

Two Communards were whispering to one side of him. Someone's rifle sights clanked together.

'Do they understand this…?' Horobenko thought. 'But what's this – a doubt? Where's it come from? Nonsense! It no longer exists and never will. You've created it yourself out of old rubbish. Bring this before your eyes once more and smash it to pieces once and for all. Be frank, Kost. You can be frank with yourself. In you (only in you, for some reason) these two forces have come together, confronting each other. From each side. You strive for equilibrium, but that is a fiction! How can they be balanced? For behind these Popelnachenkos, Krycheyevs and Druzhynins stand Spartacus, Munster, Siberia, penal servitude, strikes and October, while ahead lies the future and cycles of world tempests. And behind you, with yesterday's National Alliance and Prosvita, are the entangled strings of treachery, servility and the props of everyday theatre. How can one equate the boundless spaces of future socialism with the four walls of one's house, where "there is one's own truth, and strength, and freedom"! Step firmly forward now, Kost, and strike without missing the target. Indeed, life is built far more simply than the pretentious intelligentsia preaches it to be. Strike simply and resolutely, just like Nestorenko…!'

"Mark time… ha-a-alt!"

The detachment stopped in the middle of a clearing. People fell in line again. Once they had stopped Horobenko suddenly felt the unpleasant piercing night chillness pass through his thin shirt and prick his back. 'I should have grabbed my field jacket,' thought Horobenko and lightly stamped his feet. His cheeks were bristling from the cold and his lower jaw was beginning to tremble. 'I really should have grabbed that field jacket!'

Suddenly someone from behind threw a leather reefer over his shoulders. He turned around, and even took a step back in surprise. Popelnachenko stood before him, smiling, and said, as a good friend might have said:

"Cold, Horobenko? The reefer's for you. Take it. I've got a greatcoat."

Horobenko removed the leather jacket from his shoulders.

"No, what's this for? I'm all right…"

But Popelnachenko had already leant over and was slipping his fingers into the sleeves of his greatcoat. He grumbled angrily, even irritably:

"Stop carrying on! Put it on and let's not hear another peep out of you!"

Behind them the guards company commander, Hvozdev, called out:

"Company, right turn! Quick march!"

Nestorenko croaked nearby:

"Communist platoon, single file toward the forest, march!"

Rifle bolts clicked sharply, and feet stamped hastily.

There was no time to refuse Popelnachenko's reefer. Horobenko did up the hook on the collar and stepped into line.

Twigs crackled underfoot, bushes pushed toward him and scratched his hands. The cavalry rifle lay comfortably in Horobenko's fists and pierced the darkness.

Right in front of their line, like the wall of a hostile fortress, stood a dense, sullen copse. It was wary and silent. As if wanting to let the men come nearer still, so that it could mow them down in a single salvo. Another step forward. Two steps. Three. The scrub became thicker. Presently the copse would spray them with fire. Right this moment... Now...

They stepped over a fallen tree. Here was the first enormous oak. Its branches had become entangled in the stars and the black armour of its trunk gleamed greenly in the moonlight. The oak was threateningly silent, like a sentry on guard. 'Ah, why is it so silent…! Come on, hurry up.'

The trees moved in a wall toward them. The line of men entered the forest and quickened their step, almost running. The forest flinched and came alive. Brushwood crackled underfoot with a loud echo, and branches painfully whipped people's faces. Darkness swathed the copse and hid the line of men from view. But Horobenko could sense them all, their every irregular step. Like Horobenko, they too wanted this impossible oppressive silence to be defused, but the copse remained silent. Then feet moved more resolutely and purposely trampled the brushwood. Let there be more noise, anything to replace this silence. Anything but this silence, which perhaps up ahead concealed the levelled barrel of a rifle behind every trunk and every bush. Let those sawn-off rifles fire at last straight into their chests, only no more of this drawn-out nerve tingling waiting and the all-seeing mocking silence… the sooner they crossed this copse, the better!

Horobenko tripped over something and jumped involuntarily. He turned a little to one side, took two steps and… was rooted to the spot. Coals were burning on the ground before him… Someone had hurriedly covered the fire with earth but had failed to extinguish it. A little to one side an army kettle gleamed faintly and beside it lay a crumpled soldier's greatcoat.

Horobenko said hollowly for the rest to hear:

"There's a campfire here and a greatcoat…"

There were whispers and the line stopped.

The crackle stopped for a moment.

Horobenko stared fervently at the coals, which sorrowfully became covered in ash before his eyes and slowly died away. He itched to finger the greatcoat. They had been here just a short while ago…

Horobenko stepped onto the greatcoat and kicked the kettle. It tipped over obediently, spilling water onto Horobenko's boot.

Nestorenko hurried up on foot from behind, concerned. He greedily buried his eyes in the embers and a sharp smile filled his eyes.

BORYS ANTONENKO-DAVYDOVYCH

"There's been a nice little gang here…"

Nestorenko turned over the greatcoat with his toe, stamped about the fire, feeling the earth with his soles, and formed his hands around his mouth:

"Communist platoon! Forward, single file…"

Nestorenko raced back behind the trees.

Now, with the abandoned fire and the greatcoat behind them, it was easier going. Hands held a firm grip on rifles and feet hurried resolutely forward. Somewhere nearby horses thudded along a road. Nestorenko's voice reached them from there and became lost in the branches:

"Hvozdev! From the left flank…"

The trees thinned. The predawn sky became a pale grey. Bushes appeared again and interfered with their progress.

Suddenly a shot exploded from the right flank. It was followed by a second. And another.

"Forward, at the double!"

Another volley of shots came from the right flank. And then – silence. The line ran out of the copse onto the stubble and was catching its breath. It was already quite light. The sun was rising. Drobot appeared from somewhere, unhappy. Someone asked him a question. Drobot only waved an arm and cursed.

"…They got away."

The misty horizon receded beyond the barrow. The early morning cold scratched its way into sleeves and tickled backs.

Nestorenko and Hvozdev came galloping up from the fields. Nestorenko moved back his Kuban hat and swept the shock of hair from his forehead.

"They got away, damn it…! If I had three more horsemen I could have caught the buggers! They probably made off for the settlements."

Nestorenko sharply turned his mare around and ordered:

"Communist platoon, fall in!"

Hvozdev's tenor rang out some distance away on the ploughed field.

The detachment formed up quickly and headed toward the road.

In the distance the Vorskla River was steaming at the edge of the forest and the willows in Koziyivka loomed behind the windmills.

XXIII

There were six of them. Six of Koziyivka's wealthiest farmers. But they looked like ordinary hick peasants. Weary from work, faces finely cut by wrinkles, dishevelled beards and soiled shirts. They were phlegmatic in their movements and seemed totally indifferent. Horobenko would never have distinguished them from the poor grey masses. But Nestorenko had chosen them assiduously and painstakingly, as if seeking pedigree stallions for breeding. He spent a long time poring over lists in the village council, questioned the clerk in a lowered voice, then the taciturn stunned chairman, and then visited the houses with three Party members.

Hvozdev and his guards company had left for the settlements and Nestorenko hastened to finish with Koziyivka. He would quickly bring a hostage to the village council and hurry off to fetch the rest. Five hostages were already standing near the porch beside the Communard detachment. They stood beetle-browed and silent. None of them uttered a single word to the Party members and their bearded faces showed no fear, surprise or despair. They stood without shuffling from foot to foot, as if waiting for the authorities, who would upbraid them for unpaid taxes, for arbitrary felling of timber in the state forest and grazing stock on the landlord's meadows. Horobenko tried to look at them. He stretched out on the spurge in the shade of the village council building, lay his cavalry rifle beside him and began to roll a cigarette. However, his fingers were trembling, the tobacco spilled onto the leather pouch, and the thin cigarette paper became twisted in his fingers, not wanting to roll into a tube. An anxious feeling was growing in his chest, pressing against his heart, giving rise to a pain in his belly.

'What the hell! I'm becoming more agitated than these hostages,' Horobenko thought, and could no longer control himself. He stole a glance at the old peasants. They stood there, immobile and tight-lipped. Horobenko studied their rough, oversized boots and chapped hands and could not understand: they must know that they would answer for Harasymenko, Kirpichnikov and Feihyn, that Nestorenko hadn't dragged them from their homes to instil them with propaganda. They could not but know that! Then why this serenity? Was this prodigious stoicism or bovine stupidity...?

The square in front of the village council and the streets became empty. Only some distance away a lone pale-faced woman had frozen in fear beside a wattle fence. With twisted hands she pressed two tearful children to her skirt, as if fearing they might be taken away from her and leaned back against the fence. In some distant street a woman was screaming deliriously. The screams were so desperate, and the eyes of this woman so fearful, that it seemed as if this woman here with the children was doing the screaming and watching with her horrified eyes. The screams were like a terrible echo reflecting off a wall in that distant street and carved up Horobenko's heart. Ah, these screams, which made one's hands tremble and everything churn over in one's chest! If only these old peasants would scream too! If only they would kick, bite, punch, try to escape! Then everything would be solved of its own accord. As if deliberately, Nestorenko was delaying with the last fellow... If only he would hurry up...!

BORYS ANTONENKO-DAVYDOVYCH

Horobenko incessantly drew in on his cigarette and meanwhile the uneasiness grew in his chest, pressing up against his throat. One cigarette wasn't enough: he immediately rolled another. The sun peacefully threw wisps of light and warmth onto the square in front of the village council building. As if nothing exceptional had happened and nothing unusual was about to happen. Horobenko's forehead and neck were wet with perspiration, salty drops of dirty sweat trickled onto his lips. Meanwhile the hostages stood bare headed in the sun and did not shield themselves from it. This air of tranquillity and mundaneness brought on a sinking feeling. Horobenko thought drearily:

'Yes, this isn't the same thing as exchanging shots with a gang in the forest. This isn't war with all its revulsion. This...' and suddenly he remembered Popelnachenko's phrase uttered long ago: 'to deal with the kulaks'. This was it. What he was waiting for was drawing near, this was something he had to arrive at, but how frightening it was! They would be executed... Horobenko asked himself fearfully: 'Who...?' But there was no need for an answer. It was quite evident who was to carry out the executions...

The postmaster came out onto the square from the rural district post office, a nice-looking fellow, with a long black moustache. He slid his hands under his rope belt and calmly looked about. He was tired of postal matters and the pesky flies in the tiny room of the rural district post office and had stepped outside for a breath of fresh air.

Horobenko looked at his clean white shirt, his large forehead with no wrinkles under black hair combed to one side, and immediately it occurred to him: 'Lucky fellow! He has no one to lead, no one to guard...'

Horobenko closed his eyes for a moment and knitted his brow. 'Power keeps changing hands, first Denikin's men come here, then the Reds, then gangs, then the Reds again, but that doesn't concern him. He stamps letters, sells stamps, occasionally issues postal orders, hands out change, and in the late afternoon he goes swimming in the Vorskla River. He is left in peace by whoever is in power and he observes the events from the sidelines, as if reading the section on criminal news in newspapers from the capital. And his life is a calm inlet amid the storm of the revolution. Lucky postmaster!' And feeling just like a child, Horobenko had the strong urge to accompany the postmaster to his home and drink a glass of tea with raspberries with him…

"…With raspberries? Perhaps even listen to him play the guitar, Kost…!"

No. What was about to happen needed to happen. Life, new life, Kost, is bought with blood and secured with death. This was a new secret strict law, which could not be avoided. You know that yourself. To hell with nerves and timidity!

Kicking up a cloud of dust, they hastily brought the sixth fellow. His unbuttoned shirt revealed a small gleaming copper cross on his chest. The reddish-black, thick, moss-like beard had a stalk of straw stuck in it, like baited mice the man's small peepers darted about fearfully over the Party members. However, when he took his place beside the other hostages, he immediately calmed down and wilted, as if he had returned home after a calamity.

Nestorenko was visibly making haste. He had a quick word to Popelnachenko, ran into the village council, and a minute later raced back down the thoroughly rotted steps. He divided the Communard detachment into two groups, spoke with Popelnachenko one last time, and then turned to the hostages:

"Come on, move!"

The peasants set off obediently, like automatons.

All this happened with exceptional speed. How he found himself in the group of Communards leading the hostages out of the village and why he happened to be walking beside that sixth fellow with the copper cross – Horobenko could not remember, he could not account for it. He held his rifle at his side and tried to keep in step with the front man.

Suddenly that same insane woman's screaming pierced his chest and stabbed him painfully inside:

"Oh, help me…! Mother dear…! Symon, where are they taking you? Oh, my God…!"

A bareheaded woman was running along the street and waving her hands above her head. Her thin fingers snapped wildly and desperately, as if she was drowning and snatching at invisible threads in the air. Her lament was already affecting the rest of the convoy. The fellow in front of Horobenko transferred his rifle to the other shoulder, shook his neck and quickened his step. But the hostages remained calm, as if they could not hear the shrieks. The woman was already catching up to them. She was tearing at her hair and wailing, as if at a funeral:

"Oh, what am I to do…! Oh, my wretched life…!"

The sixth hostage finally turned around and said in a hoarse, though quite calm voice:

"Go home, Kateryna… Don't sell the stallion, but go and take the ten poods of wheat from Karpo which he borrowed from us before Easter…"

Nestorenko yelled angrily:

"Hey there – no talking!"

Someone behind them held back the woman and she began to lament even more. The old peasant turned away, sighed deeply, and continued trudging behind the others, beetle-browed and silent.

Once more Horobenko was amazed: 'Don't they realize yet? Are these live corpses or dead humans...?' He began to feel panicky walking so close to them and involuntarily fell out of step.

There was not a soul in the street, and no one was even looking from the windows. It was as if all the inhabitants had all cleared out. Only behind them, some distance away now, the woman continued her wailing, and those screams trembled in a shattered echo under the thatched eaves and clung to the branches of weeping willow.

*　　*　　*

Horobenko did not know how long they had walked. They had reached the verge of a small copse. Nestorenko himself positioned them. Carefully, so as not to make a mistake. Two paces apart. Then he moved back, shifted his Kuban hat right back and drew a large bulbous watch from his pocket.

"I'll give you another fifteen minutes... You can pray, sing, say your goodbyes – whatever you wish..." Nestorenko smiled malevolently and walked down the line of hostages.

Horobenko did not look at them. He buried his eyes in the ground and cringed.

Something heavy had rolled onto his eyelids and the crown of his head felt terribly itchy.

He felt like removing his cap and scratching himself. Oh, how itchy the crown of his head had become...! But Horobenko did not move. He stood still and limp, as if he himself was about to be executed.

Nestorenko slowly paced up and down before the silent row of old peasants and held his watch with an outstretched hand.

　　　　BORYS ANTONENKO-DAVYDOVYCH

"Ten minutes left to live… I'll knock you all off in ten minutes."

The hostages neither prayed nor said their farewells. They stood as if spellbound, silent and still. And their silence made the surroundings seem far too quiet, even eerie.

Nestorenko stopped and slowly looked at his watch.

"Eight more minutes…!"

Unexpectedly a flustered Drobot ran up to Nestorenko from somewhere and whispered into his ear. His alarmed voice was piercing, and his whispers could be heard:

"A gang is crossing the ford. You can see them from back there…"

The detachment came to life and everyone turned to face the river. Nestorenko drew his pistol and called out, as he began to run:

"Follow me…!"

They didn't have far to run to the sand dunes beyond the osier thickets. The Communards bunched together and looked intently ahead. Weaving about in all directions in the valley, the Vorskla River crept away into the distant forests. A crowd really was making its way across the ford, taking its time.

Nestorenko brought a pair of binoculars to his forehead.

"It's a herd of cows and nothing more…! Really – creating such panic…!" he remarked irritably to Drobot and turned around toward the copse.

"Follow me!"

Horobenko burst through the osier with the others. He looked, quivering, at the edge of the copse and stopped dead in his tracks. The hostages were still standing there near the copse, in the same positions… Up there near the copse six convicted men stood still, like six living deaths.

This time the Communards did not try to maintain their lines. They ran cross-country as fast as they could, as if fearing that the hostages might take to their heels any minute now and successfully escape. Before they had reached them, someone fired, and this was followed by a disorderly popping of shots. Then Horobenko saw the fellow on the end in the grey jacket roar wildly, jump to one side and dash sloppily toward the copse… Someone fell to the ground. Two more began screaming. And then a dishevelled fellow with arms spread wide apart began running straight for the Party members. Horobenko emptied his whole clip. Hastily he clicked the bolt once more. The brass casing popped out… The magazine was empty… And then suddenly he vividly saw before him… large eyes rent with terror. The small copper cross bouncing about on the shirt. A hand raised in the air. The fellow roared as he ran.

Horobenko stopped, grabbed hold of the rifle barrel, scratching his finger on the sight, and swung for all he was worth, his eyes tightly closed…

There was a thin crunch before him, and a rattling sound ensued. Something wet splashed onto Horobenko's hand. He let go of the barrel and looked. Before him a body with a smashed skull thudded hollowly onto the ground, like a scarecrow…

Shots popped on either side.

Horobenko turned around, caught his breath, and wandered off aimlessly.

He no longer heard the shouts behind him, nor the groans, nor Nestorenko's orders. He suddenly felt empty inside, and relieved in a unique kind of way.

The sun burned his forehead and his crown was still itching. He threw his cap onto the ground and was about to bury his fingers in his hair when his eyes fell on the red spot on his hand.

Blood…!

His hand began to tremble and the cherry-coloured droplet glistened in the sunshine, smiling at the sun.

All of a sudden he had a much too vivid recollection, as if it had just happened:

…Nadia's bloodied shirt and a rusty spot on the sheet… Nadia's blood! Chaste, pure virgin blood… He longed for that which had somehow disappeared, never to return, for that wreath torn asunder, and he felt tearfully overjoyed that something new had been born, something very intimate, something inseparable and dear…

*   *   *

Hastily Horobenko wiped the drop of blood on the reefer, mopped the sweat from his face, and threw his head back.

Up above, high above the earth, the azure terraces of a placid, cloudless Ukrainian sky were floating somewhere into the endless distance.

Kyiv, May 1926 – March 1927

ABOUT THE AUTHOR

Borys Antonenko-Davydovych was born on 5 August 1899 in Romny, Poltava Province, Ukraine into a working-class family. His early years were spent in Briansk, Russia. Borys learnt Ukrainian at six, after the family returned to Okhtyrka in Ukraine.

His father died in the First World War. After finishing high school in 1917, Borys left to study at Kharkiv University, then later transferred to the Kyiv Educational Institute. Though his first literary efforts were in Russian, the political struggle in Ukraine during the 1917 Revolution prompted him to start writing in Ukrainian.

His most significant early works were *Smert'* [Death, 1927; in English *Duel*, 1986], *Zemleiu ukrains'koiu* [Through Ukrainian Lands, 1929] and *Pechatka* [The Seal, 1930].

After groundless attacks in the press and accusations of nationalism, Antonenko-Davydovych was arrested in 1935 and sentenced to ten years in labour camps. He returned to Kyiv in 1956, an ailing man. Notwithstanding this, he was very active in Ukrainian literature during the 'Thaw' of the 1960s, his most popular novel of this period being *Za shyrmoiu* (*Behind the Curtain*, 1962; in English 1980). During the Brezhnev period of the 1970s he was strenuously persecuted by the authorities for his involvement in the dissident movement and his works stopped being published.

He is the author of 24 books, many of which have been translated into the languages of the former USSR.

ABOUT THE TRANSLATOR

Born in Melbourne, Australia in 1954 and educated as an engineer, **Yuri Tkacz** left the profession to translate a broad range of works from Ukrainian by such authors as Kaczurowskyj, Honchar, Dimarov, Valeriy Shevchuk, Kariuk, Vynnychenko, Yanovsky and Antonenko-Davydovych. He lived and worked in Canada in the 1980s and in Ukraine in the 1990s. His translations of *Hardly Ever Otherwise* by Maria Matios, *Hard Times* by Ostap Vyshnia, *The Lawyer from Lychakiv Street* by Andriy Kokotiukha and *Precursor* by Vasyl Shevchuk have been published by Glagoslav Publications.

ABSOLUTE ZERO

by Artem Chekh

The book is a first person account of a soldier's journey, and is based on Artem Chekh's diary that he wrote while and after his service in the war in Donbas. One of the most important messages the book conveys is that war means pain. Chekh is not showing the reader any heroic combat, focusing instead on the quiet, mundane, and harsh soldier's life. Chekh masterfully selects the most poignant details of this kind of life.

Artem Chekh (1985) is a contemporary Ukrainian writer, author of more than ten books of fiction and essays. *Absolute Zero* (2017), an account of Chekh's service in the army in the war in Donbas, is one of his latest books, for which he became a recipient of several prestigious awards in Ukraine, such as the Joseph Conrad Prize (2019), the Gogol Prize (2018), the Voyin Svitla (2018), and the Litaktsent Prize (2017). This is his first book-length translation into English.

WAR POEMS

by Alexander Korotko

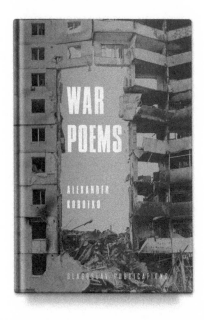

Soon after Russia invaded Ukraine on 24th February 2022, author and poet Alexander Korotko began to set down as poetry the turbulent responses at the emotional, philosophical and simply human levels evoked by the resulting war. Thus, we read in the 88 poems in this volume – completed in just less than 100 days – of the seemingly endless wail of sirens; of sheltering in cellars and tunnels; of the celebrated Ukrainian steppe, churned by tanks; the dead – "our killed, have become our Saviour Angels"; and whole poems devoted to Irpin and Mariupol as the atrocities there and elsewhere became known. Korotko is not without compassion for the Russian soldier – "Russian soldier, what did you forget in my land? We had grief enough without you." – and the soldier's mother when she receives his dead body as "cargo 200". Neither does he conceal his frustration with Ukraine's allies – "we pay the West for help with blood, but the West makes no haste to deliver."

Buy it > www.glagoslav.com

THE VILLAGE TEACHER AND OTHER STORIES

by Theodore Odrach

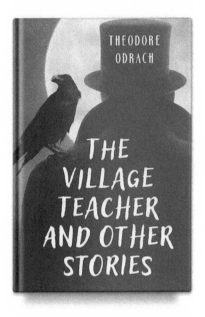

The twenty-two stories in this collection, set mostly in Eastern Europe during World War Two, depict a world fraught with conflict and chaos. Theodore Odrach is witness to the horrors that surround him, and as both an investigative journalist and a skilful storyteller, using humor and irony, he guides us through his remarkable narratives. His writing style is clean and spare, yet at the same time compelling and complex. There is no short supply of triumph and catastrophe, courage and cowardice, good and evil, as they impact the lives of ordinary people.

In "Benny's Story", a group of prisoners fight to survive despite horrific circumstances; in "Lickspittles", the absurdity of an émigré writer's life is highlighted; in "Blood", a young man travels to a distant city in search of his lost love; in "Whistle Stop", two German soldiers fight boredom in an out-of-the-way outpost, only to see their world crumble and fall.

Buy it > www.glagoslav.com

The Complete
KOBZAR
by Taras Shevchenko

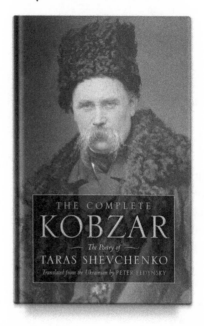

Masterfully fulfilled by Peter Fedynsky, Voice of America journalist and expert on Ukrainian studies, this first ever English translation of the complete *Kobzar* brings out Ukraine's rich cultural heritage.

As a foundational text, The *Kobzar* has played an important role in galvanizing the Ukrainian identity and in the development of Ukraine's written language and Ukrainian literature. The first editions had been censored by the Russian czar, but the book still made an enduring impact on Ukrainian culture. There is no reliable count of how many editions of the book have been published, but an official estimate made in 1976 put the figure in Ukraine at 110 during the Soviet period alone. That figure does not include Kobzars released before and after both in Ukraine and abroad. A multitude of translations of Shevchenko's verse into Slavic, Germanic and Romance languages, as well as Chinese, Japanese, Bengali, and many others attest to his impact on world culture as well.

- *Children's Fashion of the Russian Empire* by Alexander Vasiliev
- *Empire of Corruption: The Russian National Pastime* by Vladimir Soloviev
- *Heroes of the 90s: People and Money. The Modern History of Russian Capitalism* by Alexander Solovev, Vladislav Dorofeev and Valeria Bashkirova
- *Fifty Highlights from the Russian Literature* (Dutch Edition) by Maarten Tengbergen
- *Bajesvolk* (Dutch Edition) by Michail Chodorkovsky
- *Dagboek van Keizerin Alexandra* (Dutch Edition)
- *Myths about Russia* by Vladimir Medinskiy
- *Boris Yeltsin: The Decade that Shook the World* by Boris Minaev
- *A Man Of Change: A study of the political life of Boris Yeltsin*
- *Sberbank: The Rebirth of Russia's Financial Giant* by Evgeny Karasyuk
- *To Get Ukraine* by Oleksandr Shyshko
- *Asystole* by Oleg Pavlov
- *Gnedich* by Maria Rybakova
- *Marina Tsvetaeva: The Essential Poetry*
- *Multiple Personalities* by Tatyana Shcherbina
- *The Investigator* by Margarita Khemlin
- *The Exile* by Zinaida Tulub
- *Leo Tolstoy: Flight from Paradise* by Pavel Basinsky
- *Moscow in the 1930* by Natalia Gromova
- *Laurus* (Dutch edition) by Evgenij Vodolazkin
- *Prisoner* by Anna Nemzer
- *The Crime of Chernobyl: The Nuclear Goulag* by Wladimir Tchertkoff
- *Alpine Ballad* by Vasil Bykau
- *The Complete Correspondence of Hryhory Skovoroda*
- *The Tale of Aypi* by Ak Welsapar
- *Selected Poems* by Lydia Grigorieva
- *The Fantastic Worlds of Yuri Vynnychuk*
- *The Garden of Divine Songs and Collected Poetry of Hryhory Skovoroda*
- *Adventures in the Slavic Kitchen: A Book of Essays with Recipes* by Igor Klekh
- *Seven Signs of the Lion* by Michael M. Naydan

- *Forefathers' Eve* by Adam Mickiewicz
- *One-Two* by Igor Eliseev
- *Girls, be Good* by Bojan Babić
- *Time of the Octopus* by Anatoly Kucherena
- *The Grand Harmony* by Bohdan Ihor Antonych
- *The Selected Lyric Poetry Of Maksym Rylsky*
- *The Shining Light* by Galymkair Mutanov
- *The Frontier: 28 Contemporary Ukrainian Poets - An Anthology*
- *Acropolis: The Wawel Plays* by Stanisław Wyspiański
- *Contours of the City* by Attyla Mohylny
- *Conversations Before Silence: The Selected Poetry of Oles Ilchenko*
- *The Secret History of my Sojourn in Russia* by Jaroslav Hašek
- *Mirror Sand: An Anthology of Russian Short Poems*
- *Maybe We're Leaving* by Jan Balaban
- *Death of the Snake Catcher* by Ak Welsapar
- *A Brown Man in Russia* by Vijay Menon
- *Hard Times* by Ostap Vyshnia
- *The Flying Dutchman* by Anatoly Kudryavitsky
- *Nikolai Gumilev's Africa* by Nikolai Gumilev
- *Combustions* by Srđan Srdić
- *The Sonnets* by Adam Mickiewicz
- *Dramatic Works* by Zygmunt Krasiński
- *Four Plays* by Juliusz Słowacki
- *Little Zinnobers* by Elena Chizhova
- *We Are Building Capitalism! Moscow in Transition 1992-1997* by Robert Stephenson
- *The Nuremberg Trials* by Alexander Zvyagintsev
- *The Hemingway Game* by Evgeni Grishkovets
- *A Flame Out at Sea* by Dmitry Novikov
- *Jesus' Cat* by Grig
- *Want a Baby and Other Plays* by Sergei Tretyakov
- *Mikhail Bulgakov: The Life and Times* by Marietta Chudakova
- *Leonardo's Handwriting* by Dina Rubina
- *A Burglar of the Better Sort* by Tytus Czyżewski
- *The Mouseiad and other Mock Epics* by Ignacy Krasicki
- *Ravens before Noah* by Susanna Harutyunyan

- *An English Queen and Stalingrad* by Natalia Kulishenko
- *Point Zero* by Narek Malian
- *Absolute Zero* by Artem Chekh
- *Olanda* by Rafał Wojasiński
- *Robinsons* by Aram Pachyan
- *The Monastery* by Zakhar Prilepin
- *The Selected Poetry of Bohdan Rubchak: Songs of Love, Songs of Death, Songs of the Moon*
- *Mebet* by Alexander Grigorenko
- *The Orchestra* by Vladimir Gonik
- *Everyday Stories* by Mima Mihajlović
- *Slavdom* by Ľudovít Štúr
- *The Code of Civilization* by Vyacheslav Nikonov
- *Where Was the Angel Going?* by Jan Balaban
- *De Zwarte Kip* (Dutch Edition) by Antoni Pogorelski
- *Głosy / Voices* by Jan Polkowski
- *Sergei Tretyakov: A Revolutionary Writer in Stalin's Russia* by Robert Leach
- *Opstand* (Dutch Edition) by Władysław Reymont
- *Dramatic Works* by Cyprian Kamil Norwid
- *Children's First Book of Chess* by Natalie Shevando and Matthew McMillion
- *Precursor* by Vasyl Shevchuk
- *The Vow: A Requiem for the Fifties* by Jiří Kratochvil
- *De Bibliothecaris* (Dutch edition) by Mikhail Jelizarov
- *Subterranean Fire* by Natalka Bilotserkivets
- *Vladimir Vysotsky: Selected Works*
- *Behind the Silk Curtain* by Gulistan Khamzayeva
- *The Village Teacher and Other Stories* by Theodore Odrach
- *Duel* by Borys Antonenko-Davydovych
- *War Poems* by Alexander Korotko
- *The Revolt of the Animals* by Wladyslaw Reymont
- *Liza's Waterfall: The Hidden Story of a Russian Feminist* by Pavel Basinsky
- *Biography of Sergei Prokofiev* by Igor Vishnevetsky
  More coming . . .

GLAGOSLAV PUBLICATIONS
www.glagoslav.com